W9-BVT-959

LOULY

by Carol Ryrie Brink

ILLUSTRATED BY INGRID FETZ

Macmillan Publishing Co., Inc.
NEW YORK
Collier Macmillan Publishers
LONDON

Copyright © 1974 Carol Ryrie Brink
Copyright © 1974 Macmillan Publishing Co., Inc.
All rights reserved. No part of this book may be reproduced or
transmitted in any form or by any means, electronic or mechanical,
including photocopying, recording or by any information storage
and retrieval system, without permission in writing from the Publisher.
Macmillan Publishing Co., Inc.
866 Third Avenue, New York, N.Y. 10022
Collier-Macmillan Canada Ltd.
Printed in the United States of America

1   2   3   4   5   6   7   8   9   10

Library of Congress Cataloging in Publication Data
Brink, Carol (Ryrie), date   Louly.

I. Fetz, Ingrid, illus.   II. Title.
PZ7.B78Lo   [Fic]   73–21885   ISBN 0–02–713680–9

JF
B858l

For Nora
with love

Contents

1 · The Play-like Plays

Louly was beginning to grow up that summer of 1908. She had always been pretty and full of ideas, but suddenly she was prettier than ever and the ideas popped out all over her.

Her mother noticed it and said to her father, "She's almost fifteen and she's getting to be very responsible. I think we might leave her in charge and take that trip Back East that we have been hoping for."

The boys up and down the street noticed it, and sometimes they whistled as Louly went by.

Chrys and Cordy noticed it with rather sour expressions on their faces. The old Louly was very important to their plays, and this summer the plays were a very important part of their lives.

Louly's brother, Ko-Ko, who was sixteen, and her sister, Poo-Bah, who was ten, were the only ones who did not notice that Louly was growing up. They saw her every day, and she looked just the same to them, winter or summer, rain or shine.

Louly had wide gray eyes and soft brown hair that escaped in little curls around her face no matter how severely she tied it back. But it was not so much the color of eyes and hair as the liveliness of her face that mattered. She looked as if she were always on the verge of discovering something wonderful.

The Tucker family had come to live next door to Chrys and her aunt and grandmother two years ago when Chrys was eleven and Louly was thirteen, and in spite of the difference in ages the girls had become friends immediately. The Tuckers were shared by Cordy too, because they had come from the same town in Michigan where Cordy's family had lived and they knew all of the same people Back East. Everyone in Idaho seemed to come from somewhere "Back East." To hear people talk, Chrys thought, she must be the only one who had ever been born in Idaho. She had never been east of the Rocky Mountains, and the nearest relatives outside of Idaho that she had were far away in Scotland. But Cordy and Louly had grandparents and aunts and uncles and "cousins by the dozens," as Louly said, back in Michigan. It was boring sometimes to hear them talk.

However there were not many times when the girls sat around and talked. Mostly they did things, like sewing up aprons from bandana handkerchiefs, or pasting scrapbooks of long-necked beauties from magazine covers, or making fudge, or running down to the bakery for cinnamon rolls, or to the ice-cream parlor for pineapple ice-cream sodas. There was always something going on around Louly. And then there were the plays.

During the winter there had been a stock company of actors in town, and almost every Saturday afternoon the girls had gone to the matinee to see a different play, *Charley's Aunt* and *Uncle Tom's Cabin*, *Trilby* and *East Lynne*. When the stock company left town at the end of the season, there was a sudden lag in entertainment. That was when the girls had started to make up their own plays.

It was early evening on the first hot night of spring, and they were playing Living Statues on the lawn at Chrys's house. Living Statues is a tiresome game in which the person who is IT takes each player in turn and twirls him around and tosses him aside, and whatever position the player lands in he must hold like a living statue, until everybody has been twirled and has landed and become immobilized. It might be fun if you could see how everybody else looked; but if you have landed on a heel and one elbow with the other leg in the air and the other arm behind your head, you are not in a very good position to look around and laugh at the funny positions the other players have assumed. After a while the game gets dull. Next they had tried Starving Time in Virginia and everybody tried to see who could look the most starved with cheeks sucked in and knees drawn up. But after a good dinner this was difficult, too, and not very amusing.

They all sat silent on the cool grass, thinking, and then Louly said,

"Let's give a real play—I mean a *real* one, like the stock company plays."

"How?" asked Cordy.

"But you have to have a book and learn parts," objected Chrys.

"Not at all," said Louly in her lofty tone. "You take a story everybody knows, and you assign parts, and maybe you just sketch out scenes or divide it into acts, and then you go ahead and make up your own words and you *do* it."

"I speak to be the fairy godmother," piped Poo-Bah. Poo-Bah had to look after her own rights. She had played with three older girls long enough to know that nothing was gained by remaining silent.

"Who said we are going to have a fairy godmother?" inquired Cordy.

"Yes, who did?" asked Chrys.

"Well, you never know," said Poo-Bah. "Anyway, I've spoken for it."

"We *might* have a fairy godmother," said Louly, "and then we might *not*. We all know fairy tales. We could start with one of those. It would be easier than *East Lynne* or *Uncle Tom*."

"How about 'Red Riding Hood?'" suggested Cordy. She was thinking fast to try to remember if there was a red cape in one of her mother's trunks in the attic at home.

"I speak to be the wolf," cried Poo-Bah.

"I think something more romantical," said Chrys dreamily.

"Yes," decided Louly, "something more romantical like 'Beauty and the Beast' or . . . ."

"I speak to be the Beast!"

". . . Or 'Sleeping Beauty.' "

" 'Sleeping Beauty!' " they all cried. "That's the one!"

"Then what shall I speak to be?" cried Poo-Bah, trying hard to remember the juiciest parts in "Sleeping Beauty."

"You can be the wicked fairy who comes to the christening, honey," said Louly indulgently. "I will be the prince because I am the tallest, and Cordy is next tallest, so she can be my squire or my jester or something like that."

"And what about me?" asked Chrys.

"Why, you—you can be the beautiful princess."

"Oh, dear," said Chrys, "I always have to be something dull like that. I wish I could grow enough to be a prince or a villain or a murderer or something."

"You ought to be mighty thankful to be the leading lady," Louly said.

Chrys understood the logic which decreed that the tallest girls should get the most adventurous parts.

"All right," she said.

"And, of course," continued Louly, "we'll all have to double on the other parts—the king and queen, and the good fairy, and the guardian of the tower, and so forth."

Chrys's front yard was ideal for plays, because it had lots of space and the big trees could easily be imagined as enchanted woods. The action started down in the corner of the yard nearest the street, where the tall picket fence and the posts with balls on top could be imagined as crenelated castle walls. From there the scenes ranged all over the lawn and came to a climax at the hammock under the crab-apple trees, which made an excellent sleeping place in a bewitched forest.

When the play started, the last bits of late sunshine were sifting through the leaves and falling like scattered golden coins on the deep green of the grass. As it continued, the sun faded and was replaced by a mysterious twilight, and then the moon (or was it the corner street lamp?) began to scatter silver coins on the black-velvet lawn. The girls drifted through the story of the Sleeping Beauty as if it had been a beautiful dream—a dream that all four shared. Occasionally Louly stopped them, and said: "No, that was all wrong. It ought to go like this. Play like you do this and Cordy does that, and Poo-Bah says 'Zounds!' and we'll all go on from there, and it will turn out right this time."

No one doubted Louly's wisdom or authority. She was always speaking pieces at school and Sunday School, and once she had had a real part in a pageant in the town hall. Sleeping Beauty turned out to be a lovely play, and they were all satisfied. It was bedtime by the time it was finished. The four girls sat on the lowest step of Chrys's front porch and thought it over in silence. There was a magic spell in the air that no one wanted to break. Then from next door Mrs. Tucker called, "Louly! Poo-Bah! Time to come in now."

A long sigh went up from the players.

"Mama," Louly called, "we'll be there in a minute. We've got to walk Cordy home past the courthouse."

"Well, you and Chrys walk her home as fast as you can. But Poo-Bah must come in at once. Hurry now."

They hurried slowly, still in the lovely dream. At the courthouse that stood halfway between Chrys's and Cordy's houses, they bade Cordy good night.

The courthouse was a big square building that contained the county jail, and sometimes the prisoners looked out of the barred windows. It was scary to pass it alone at night, so the girls liked to have company as long as possible. Tonight everything was calm and quiet.

"Run now," Louly said, "and Chrys and I will wait until you reach your back fence in case you scream for help or anything."

"All right," Cordy said as she began to run.

There were no screams for help and Louly and Chrys strolled slowly homeward.

"I thought it was a beautiful play," Chrys said.

"Yes," agreed Louly, "and we can have lots more. There are all kinds of stories besides fairy tales. All we need is for all of us to know the story so we don't have to waste time telling it over to each other."

"*Little Women,* maybe?" Chrys said.

"Uh-huh. Or *Mrs. Wiggs of the Cabbage Patch.*"

"*Black Beauty?*"

"No, it's too complicated if we have to have animals."

"Poo-Bah would speak to be the horse," said Chrys with a chuckle. The rest of the way home they were silent.

That summer Chrys slept on a cot on a little screened porch at the back of her grandmother's house. It was all her own place and nobody disturbed her. A big honey locust tree, full of white, scented blossoms, hung over the sleeping porch and let moonlight come seeping through the leaves onto her face as she slept. Under her bed Chrys kept a shoe box with some of her very personal and secret treasures, like the diary Cordy had given her on her birthday and the letter from Mr. Banks that had

come from far-off Wisconsin where he was spend-
ing the summer with his family, and the ring
shaped like a snake with a green stone eye that she
had found on the way home from town one day.
There were a spelling tablet and a well-sharpened
stub of a pencil in the shoe box too. The spelling
tablet was no longer used for such a tiresome business as spelling. In it Chrys had written three
poems, one about trees and one about kittens and
one about falling snow. She had never shown the
poems to any person in the world, not even to
Cordy. She did not know whether they were good or
not, but they were hers, her own, and she was not
ready to share them with anybody.

Before she undressed, Chrys lighted a stub of
candle that sat in a saucer on the orange crate
beside her bed. She sat on her bed and read over
her three poems, and then she began to write on a
fresh page of the spelling tablet.

> *Ah, lovely moonlight*
> *Shining bright*
> *Sleeping Beauty woke tonight.*
> *Even if 'twas but a play*
> *I am glad it was this way*
> *What an ending for a day!*

It was not very good, she thought. How did you put all of the mystery and fun of the evening into a poem and make it rhyme? Maybe tomorrow she could improve it. She put it into the shoe box and put the shoe box under the bed, and presently she undressed and went to sleep with the moonlight shining on her face.

After that there were plays almost every day or evening. Vacation started and the days were very long and golden. The girls all had chores to do in the mornings, but then they would gather on Chrys's front or side porch, and say, "What shall we do?" Then Louly would say: "Listen! Let's play like—" and in a few moments they would be off on some familiar story. Louly could speak in many voices. She could be haughty as a princess, snarling as a villain, dignified and deep-toned as a judge. If she wished to make a good impression, she put on her Southern accent and drawled "yo' all" and "sho' nuff" and "Ah decla'e to goodness!" It was a marvel to listen to her. The others all began to imitate her, and it was strange and exciting.

Once you decided what character you were going to be, your voice changed and you began speaking like that character. If you were a queen you raised your eyebrows and shoulders and walked with a stately tread. You spoke in haughty and measured tones. If you were an old crone, you bent half-double and spoke in a quavering falsetto. If you were a prince your voice was deep and you strutted and laid about you with your sword. The only thing the three younger girls did not try to imitate was Louly's Southern accent. That was not for plays but only to impress people, and it made them self-conscious and uncomfortable.

Ko-Ko laughed at them when he saw them parading around and mouthing fancy speeches. But then Ko-Ko was usually over at the Larks' house doing things with Cordy's four brothers, so he was really no great trouble to the girls.

Ko-Ko's real name was Conrad, but when he was small he had got the nickname Ko-Ko. Mr. and Mrs. Tucker had met when they had parts in a high school production of *The Mikado*. Mrs. Tucker had sung the part of Yum-Yum and Mr. Tucker had been Ko-Ko, the Lord High Executioner. Now Mr. Tucker was the principal of the high school, and he and Mrs. Tucker only sang around the piano at home or in the church choir. But when Conrad was born, it had seemed very easy to nickname him Ko-Ko after the Lord High Executioner, and Paula Belle had soon become Poo-Bah, who was the Lord High Everything Else in *The Mikado*.

"And why didn't you call me Yum-Yum?" Louly wanted to know.

"Well, but your name is Louisa Lee," Mrs. Tucker said. "What else could we call you but Louly?"

"But why do we have to have nicknames?" Poo-Bah wanted to know. "I think that Paula Belle is much more beautiful than Poo-Bah."

"Oh, I don't know," Mrs. Tucker said. "Nicknames mean that we love you, I suppose. Did you ever hear of an unloved person called by a nickname?"

"There's Fatty Hammerschnickle," Poo-Bah said. "I doubt if anybody loves him."

"Oh, dear!" Mrs. Tucker said, "you children will be the death of me yet!"

2 · Baking-Powder Biscuits

It was well on toward the end of June when Mr. and Mrs. Tucker decided to go Back East for a visit. Mrs. Tucker's mother, Mrs. Louisa Lee, after whom Louly was named, had had a heart attack. It was not a very serious one, but it made Mrs. Tucker think that she really should go back to see her mother and all the "cousins by the dozens" before it was too late.

"But I don't see how we can possibly afford to take the children," Mr. Tucker said. "Poo-Bah could still go for half fare on the train, but Ko-Ko and Louly would have to have full-fare tickets, and there are all the meals in the diner and everything."

"We will leave them here," Mrs. Tucker said. "Ko-Ko is very serious and responsible, and Louly is growing up. She's getting quite dependable, and she is learning to cook."

"Her *fudge* is excellent," said Mr. Tucker with a wry smile.

"I think the responsibility will be good for them," Mrs. Tucker said. "Poo-Bah can help, too, and the older ones can look after her. We would only be gone a month or six weeks, and I'm sure that Chrys's grandmother and aunt could be relied on in emergencies and Cordy Lark's people are only a few blocks away. I'll call Mrs. Lark right now and then I'll go over and talk to Chrys's aunt."

Cordy and Chrys, Louly and Poo-Bah sat in a row on Chrys's side porch. There was no railing on the side porch and their feet hung down at various lengths ending in bare toes, for it was a lovely, bare-foot day. Beyond the fence and driveway was the

Tuckers' house, and Mrs. Tucker had just run over to talk with Chrys's Aunt Eugenia, who was baking cookies. The side porch opened off the kitchen and the four girls could hear everything that was said.

"I do so much want to see my dear mother again," Mrs. Tucker was saying. Her voice floated out of the kitchen along with the spicy smell of fresh cookies. The four girls listened and sniffed at the same time.

"You certainly should go," Aunt Eugenia said. "I'm sure the children will be all right."

"Louly is growing up," Mrs. Tucker said. "She's getting quite dependable."

Louly raised her shoulders and her eyebrows and put on the haughty queen look. Poo-Bah mouthed a silent "Ha! Ha! Ha!" Chrys and Cordy grinned.

"We will leave them money to run the house and pay the bills, and the vegetable garden beyond the sweet pea fence is coming along nicely. There are lettuce and radishes and green onions, and later there will be corn and beans and tomatoes and peas —that is, if they take care of it. The children will be absolutely self-sufficient. Only I just thought—in case of emergencies . . . !"

"I understand perfectly," Aunt Eugenia said. "They'll get along just fine, but if the slightest emergency arises, they can always call on us and Mother and I will do everything we can to help them. You can rely on that."

"I hope there will be no emergencies."

"Oh, of course there won't be. What could happen here in summertime anyway?"

At this Poo-Bah slipped off the porch and fell into a swoon, muttering "Emergency! Emergency!"

"Get up, silly," hissed Louly. "You don't want to scare them out of going now by acting an emergency. We'll have a lot of fun."

"Do you really want them to go Back East and leave you all alone here?" asked Cordy.

"Yes," Louly said. "They want so much to see Grandma Lee and all the other relatives, and think what fun we'll have doing everything ourselves, and just how and when we want to do it."

"Gee, yes!" the others said, beginning to envision a whole new way of life.

Poo-Bah climbed back on the porch. "We can sleep just as long as we like in the mornings, and not practice piano and not go to Sunday School and have fudge every day for lunch instead of soup and—"

"No," Louly said, "I have to be dependable, and I *will* be. We'll do everything the way our father and mother would do it—as nearly as we can, that is. But we'll also have fun—a lot of fun!"

The other girls looked at Louly with admiration. Yes, Louly was dependable and they knew that when she said they would have fun, they would have fun.

Chrys and Cordy went along with the Tucker children to see Mr. and Mrs. Tucker leave on the train. Mrs. Tucker wanted it that way, "so they won't be too lonesome by themselves when they see the train pulling out," she said.

Actually, now that the time for departure had come, it seemed to be Mrs. Tucker who minded the parting most. Mr. Tucker was busy with tickets and luggage, and the children were all thinking of the good time Louly had promised them when they were alone.

Mrs. Tucker said, "Oh, dear! I *hope* it will all work out. I don't know why I ever thought of going and leaving you—"

"We'll be fine, Mother," Louly said.

"Remember not to let the ice run out in the icebox, and keep the lawn mowed and watered and weed the sweet peas, Ko-Ko."

"I'll remember, Mother," Ko-Ko said.

"And, Louly, when you open a can of beef or soup, be sure that the can does not bulge. That's a sure sign that it's contaminated."

"But they never bulge, Mama darling," Louly said.

"Promise you will look, dear, anyhow."

"I promise."

"And Poo-Bah, dearest Poo-Bah, you'll always clean your teeth and say your prayers, won't you, darling?"

"Yes, I will, Mother," Poo-Bah promised.

"And, Cordy and Chrys, you'll look after my loved ones, won't you? You won't let them get lonesome or into trouble, will you?"

"We'll be there every day in case of emergencies," cried Cordy and Chrys.

After that there was much kissing all around and shaking of hands between Mr. Tucker and Ko-Ko. Then the conductor was shouting "All-l-l-l-l aboard!" and the parents were inside the train and looking out of the window. Slowly the train began to move, and the children ran along beside it to the end of the platform, waving and throwing kisses.

There was only one unnerving thing. The last they saw of Mrs. Tucker through the train window she was weeping into her handkerchief, and Mr. Tucker was putting his arm around her to comfort her.

The five young people stood on the end of the platform watching the train as it picked up speed and went roaring away through the wheat fields.

Soon it was lost in the folds of the rolling hills. Even its smoke vanished before the children turned back toward town.

"She was crying," Poo-Bah said. "Did you see it? Mama was crying. She didn't want to go and leave us after all." Suddenly Poo-Bah herself burst into tears.

"Oh, dear!" cried Louly. "Who's got a handkerchief? Quick!" Nobody had one, and Poo-Bah had to wipe her eyes on the back of her hand.

They all stood around her and watched her cry. Was this an emergency? Chrys wondered uneasily. Then Louly knelt down and put her arms around Poo-Bah.

"Listen, Lovey," she said, "it's only for a month or six weeks. We'll get along somehow. Don't you cry now, Poo-Bah."

Poo-Bah cried harder than ever. Everyone tried to comfort her, and no one succeeded.

"You said it was going to be f-f-un," murmured Poo-Bah reproachfully through her tears. The three older girls looked at each other, and tears began running down all of their cheeks.

Ko-Ko was disgusted.

"You'd think that the train had already been wrecked and we were never going to see them again," he remarked coldly.

"The train is going to be wrecked, and we're never going to see them again," cried Poo-Bah with fresh torrents of tears.

"He didn't say that, darling," said Louly, "he only said—oh, dear!"

"Oh, shut up!" said Ko-Ko rudely. "You girls are acting like a bunch of ninnies. What's the matter with you? Look here!" He reached in his pocket and drew out a silver dollar. It was round and quite shiny. They all looked at it and Poo-Bah stopped crying.

"Where did you get that?" she said.

"Father gave it to me the very last thing. 'It's for ice-cream sodas,' he said, 'in case the girls cry or anything. You can treat them.' "

"Ice-cream sodas!" cried Poo-Bah and Louly.

"Us too?" asked Cordy and Chrys.

"All of us," said Ko-Ko. "Now dry up and let's have no more tears the rest of the summer. Is that clear?"

No one promised anything about tears for the rest of the summer, but as they walked uptown to the ice-cream parlor they grew more and more cheerful.

The four girls sat around one of the small gilt tables on the gilt chairs of twisted wire. Ko-Ko sat by himself at the counter in case some of his friends should come in and catch him sitting with little girls and sisters. But he was near enough to hear all they were saying, and he put the dollar down on the marble counter with quite a clink, as if it were his own treat.

"What kind of ice-cream sodas would you like?" asked Mr. Childers, the ice-cream man.

"Pineapple, please," said Chrys.

"Chocolate," said Cordy.

"Sarsaparilla," said Louly with raised eyebrows and her little finger elegantly crooked.

"Do you ever mix flavors, Mr. Childers?" asked Poo-Bah.

"Well, we could," said Mr. Childers.

"Then I will have strawberry and cherry, please. Very well mixed."

"Ick!" said Ko-Ko from his high stool by the counter. He was having plain vanilla.

Chrys had a ritual for getting the most enjoyment out of her ice-cream soda. First she ate the fuzz off the top with her spoon, then she ate the ice cream before it melted, then she sucked up all the soda with her straw, and finally she made a loud noise sucking air through the straw after all the soda was gone.

Cordy proceeded in an entirely different manner, sucking out the soda first and eating the ice cream from the bottom of the glass with the long spoon at the last.

They were all happily occupied for some time. They sat on for a little while, putting off the moment when they would go home to an empty house.

But at last Louly said, "Come on, kidlets, let's go." When Louly called the others "kidlets," she was being very grown-up and responsible. They all got up and began walking slowly up the hill to the Tuckers' house.

Billy, the Tuckers' collie dog, was lying on the front porch, and that was reassuring. Ko-Ko unlocked the front door and they all went in and sat around the parlor looking at each other.

"I think I'll go over to the Larks'," said Ko-Ko. "I'll be back in time for supper."

"What *is* for supper?" asked Poo-Bah.

"Mother left cold ham and potato salad in the icebox," Louly said, "and I think that I shall make hot baking-powder biscuits."

"How about fudge?" asked Poo-Bah.

"No, honey," Louly said in a motherly voice. "Fudge is a waste of sugar and bad for the teeth, and I'm going to make wonderful baking-powder biscuits."

"Ham and salad and biscuits," observed Chrys. "It sounds mighty good to me, Poo-Bah."

"Listen, Chrys," said Louly. "Why don't you run

and ask your aunt if you can stay? And Cordy can call up her mother. It will be much less lonesome the first meal if you keep us company."

"Fine," said Chrys, dashing away to ask her aunt, and Cordy was already cranking up the telephone.

"You see, we really ought to keep them company," Chrys said to her aunt. "It's our duty, really, I think."

"Well, if you're sure that Louly wants you. They could come over here, you know."

"No, Louly's cooking. It's going to be very, very good."

When Chrys returned to the Tuckers', Louly was in the kitchen consulting recipes and clattering pans. She had built up a fire in the cookstove so that the oven would be hot in time for the biscuits. Cordy had permission to remain and she and Poo-Bah were sitting on the woodbox being very helpful with suggestions and advice. Chrys joined them.

"I love your mother's biscuits," she said, "they're so nice and light and fluffy."

"Uh-huh," said Louly absently. She wasn't sure whether she should sift the flour before or after she measured it. Cordy thought *before* and Chrys thought *afterward*. They had a lot to say about it.

"Go set the table, kidlets," Louly said at last. "It's kind of hard to concentrate when all of you are saying different things."

They set the table and brought in a bouquet of sweet peas for the centerpiece. Then they all helped Louly cut out the biscuits and put them in the pan.

"They look a little hard and flat," said Chrys.

"That's perfectly normal," said Cordy. "They don't begin to rise until you put them in the oven."

Louly looked thoughtful. "I hope I got everything in all right," she said.

Ko-Ko came back at six o'clock hungry as a bear. When he saw that Cordy and Chrys were still there, he said, "Well, I see that I'm going to have a harem this summer."

"All right," Louly said. "Someday you can ask all of the Lark boys over for a meal, and I'll cook it for you."

"I'll try your cooking first," said Ko-Ko skeptically.

The plates of cold ham and potato salad came out of the icebox, looking fresh and delicious. Mrs. Tucker had even decorated the ham with bits of parsley and the potato salad with wedges of hard-boiled egg and a sprinkling of paprika.

"You sit in Daddy's place," said Louly to Ko-Ko, "and I'll sit in Mother's, and you may serve."

"All right," said Ko-Ko, "but where are the biscuits?"

"Oh, the biscuits!" cried Louly and ran to the kitchen. She was gone quite a long time. Ko-Ko had time to serve ham and salad on all five plates.

"Hurry up, Lou," he called.

"I'm coming," Louly said.

When she came in she was carrying a plate covered with a napkin. "Here they are," she said. "They're a little too brown and something else is wrong. I don't know what."

"Let's see! Let's see!"

Louly lifted the napkin and everybody looked.

"They're just as flat as when they went into the oven," Cordy said.

"But your mother's biscuits were always so light and fluffy," remarked Chrys.

"Ick!" said Ko-Ko.

"I think," said Louly miserably, "I think I must have left out the baking powder."

"But how could you do that?" cried Cordy. "When you make baking-powder biscuits, I should think the first thing you would put in would be the baking powder!"

"Actually it is the last thing," Louly said, "and you were all talking to me and—"

"The proof is in the eating," said Ko-Ko, reaching

for a biscuit. "Ouch! It's hot! And it's as hard as a rock! Jumping Jehoshaphat! What a cook!"

Louly flung down her napkin and ran upstairs to her room.

"Now see what you've done!" said Poo-Bah. "You've gone and hurt her feelings."

"Shall we go after her?" asked Chrys.

"I'll go," Ko-Ko said. "It's my fault, and listen, you kids, get busy and start to eat those biscuits."

"They really aren't bad," Cordy said, after the first heroic mouthful, "they're kind of crispish-like."

"Unleavened bread," said Chrys. "Haven't I read about unleavened bread somewhere?"

"What's unleavened bread?" asked Poo-Bah.

"It's bread without yeast or baking powder, I think," said Chrys.

After a while Ko-Ko and Louly came downstairs. Louly's eyes were red, but she was being firmly reliable.

"She just wanted to get a handkerchief," explained Ko-Ko.

The others were all munching biscuits at great peril to their teeth.

"They're really good, Louly," Cordy said; and "I think you've invented something new," said Chrys.

"I'll do better next time," Louly said.

"Louly," asked Poo-Bah, "when are we going to

begin to have fun?" It was not exactly the right moment for the question, but Louly smiled bravely.

"Tomorrow," she said.

"What are we going to do?"

"We are going camping," Louly said.

"*Camping?*" the other girls cried in astonishment.

"*Camping?*" yelped Ko-Ko.

"Certainly," said Louly calmly. "Why not?"

"You know why not," said Ko-Ko. "Mother and Dad would have a fit if we went to the mountains all by ourselves. I might go, of course, but certainly not you girls."

"Who mentioned the mountains?" asked Louly.

"Well, but how——?"

"In the backyard," Louly said. "There's a perfectly splendid place for the tent. I don't know why we never thought of trying it before."

3 · Magic Forest

First thing the next morning Louly sent Ko-Ko to
the attic for the tent. It had not been used since last
summer when the family spent a week camping in
the mountains.

Ko-Ko was skeptical. "I'll help you put it up," he
said, "but you girls will have to sleep in it. I'm going
to sleep in my nice comfortable bed."

"Sissy!" said Poo-Bah.

"And don't expect me to come and rescue you when the bears begin to prowl around at night."

"*Bears?*"

"Don't pay any attention to him, honey," Louly said. "He's probably talking about squirrels, and they won't bother us."

Chrys and Cordy arrived as soon after breakfast as they could possibly get away from home, and they were in time for almost everything. Louly and Ko-Ko had just spread the tent out on the back lawn between the box-elder tree and the sweet-pea fence, and Poo-Bah was carrying the box of tent pegs and extra ropes.

Behind Chrys came her Aunt Eugenia and her grandmother. Rowdy, her dog, came too, and he and Billy began to race around the lawn and put on a sham battle. They were really very good friends.

"Well, this looks interesting," Grandma said. "Reminds me of the time my brothers and I tried to put up an Indian tepee in the farmyard in Wisconsin. But it kept falling down. We weren't quite Indians enough to make it work. You've got a good modern tent, however, and it looks as if it might go up quite easily."

"Oh, dear!" Aunt Eugenia said, "I don't know whether we should let you do this. I promised your mother that we would look out for your safety."

"In case of emergencies, Aunt," reminded Chrys.

"Maybe we should have asked you first," said Louly, "but it seemed like a good idea and we never thought."

"I think it's a fine idea," said Grandma. "How many of you are going to sleep out?"

"Not me!" said Ko-Ko. "I'll help them put up the tent, but I like my own bed."

"All four girls," said Cordy. "Mama's given her permission."

"And Billy too," Louly said.

"It sounds safe enough," Grandma said in a businesslike voice. "Well, why don't you get on with it? You'll have to put the poles up first, and you'll need some mosquito netting over the flap. How do you intend to do your cooking?"

"Well, we were going to ask you about that," said Louly. "Over an open fire, I thought."

"Cook out?" cried Poo-Bah. "You mean we're going to cook *outdoors*?"

"No more biscuits," said Ko-Ko under his breath.

"Oh, joy!" cried Chrys and Cordy, hugging each other.

"Oh, this is terrible," Aunt Eugenia said. "You might burn down both houses, and the Tuckers would come home to find nothing but charred ruins and all of their children in bandages."

"Nonsense," Grandma said. "Did you ever build a furnace?" she asked the children.

"*I* know how," said Ko-Ko, showing his first sign of lively interest. "First you dig a small pit, and you put some bricks on the sides of it with a piece of metal across the top, leaving an open space at the front and a small hole at the back—"

"A piece of old stovepipe is better at the back," Grandma said. "It carries away the smoke and makes a good draft. The cooking is cleaner and more comfortable that way. The fire can all be kept in the dirt pit, and it's quite safe if sensible children use reasonable care."

"We'll be very careful," Louly promised.

"And, come to think of it," Grandma said, "I just happen to have a piece of old stovepipe in the woodshed that you could use. It has a joint in it, and if you turn it in the right direction it will carry the smoke away and keep it out of the cook's eyes."

"Oh, good!" they cried.

Aunt Eugenia sighed and then she began to smile. "And I have an old frying pan with a long handle that doesn't get hot easily. I don't mind lending it to you."

"Good! Good!"

"Well," Grandma said, "get the tent up and build

the furnace and when it's all done I'll be glad to come out and inspect it for safety."

"Oh, thanks!" cried Louly. "And maybe we'll invite you to a camp dinner sometime. I promise not to make baking-powder biscuits."

The five campers had never worked harder in their lives. The tent went up and was neatly pegged out. There was much perspiring and shouting and arguing, but everybody had a wonderful time.

The furnace was something else and required a lot of planning and discussion. It couldn't be dug in the middle of the lawn, and it shouldn't be too near anything that might catch fire or too far away from the tent. There was a driveway between Chrys's house and the Tuckers' house. Halfway along, the drive turned into Chrys's side gate and went on to her grandma's barn where she kept her pony and cart. The Tuckers did not have a barn or a horse, but a piece of the driveway continued on past Chrys's gate toward the Tuckers' back shed, where a horse might once have been kept. Now the shed held a lawn mower, garden tools, some old boxes and packing cases, and a pile of unused bricks.

When Ko-Ko went to the shed to look at the bricks, he got an idea for the location of the furnace.

"Look here, kids!" he said. "How about this end of the old driveway? Nobody uses it to drive on and it's not too far from the tent. We won't have to spoil any grass to dig the hole."

"Is it safe?" asked Louly anxiously.

"We don't need to put it near the shed. Come and see. It looks all right to me."

They all came and looked at the spot Ko-Ko pointed out, and there was general approval.

By the time they had begun to dig, Cordy's brothers Matt and Vince arrived. Matt was about Ko-Ko's age and Vince was about the age of Poo-Bah.

"What goes on here?" asked Matt.

"These crazy loons are planning to camp out," said Ko-Ko loftily.

"Then why are *you* digging?" asked Matt.

"I'm just helping them a little," Ko-Ko said. "You know how helpless girls are!"

"Don't be silly!" said Louly. "I dug the first shovelful myself and that's the hardest. We're all taking turns."

"Can I take a turn too, say?" shouted Vince.

"We might let you," Louly said, "after all of us have had a turn. It's really fun."

"That's a swell tent you've got there," said Matt. "But what are you doing *here*?"

"We're making a furnace," Cordy said. "What does it look like?"

"It looks like a little, small hole in a hard driveway."

"We're going to cook out," said Louly. "All kinds of delicious things."

"Like what?"

"Well, bacon and eggs and raw fries."

"Raw fries?" cried everyone. "What's that?"

"You don't know raw fries?" said Louly in astonishment. "You take raw potatoes and you slice them up in hot bacon fat and you fry them until they are crisp and brown and you put a little salt on them, and are they ever delicious! My favorite food!"

"But *raw* fries, Louly!" protested Chrys.

"They aren't raw after they're fried, of course," said Louly. "Wait until you taste them."

With the thought of crisp brown fried potatoes in mind, they all dug harder than ever. Matt and Vince took their turns, and it soon looked as if the hole were going to be a well.

"Stop! Stop!" Louly cried. "We've got to think this over. How big is the top of our furnace going to be?"

"Just big enough to hold a frying pan, I should think," said Cordy.

"Do we *have* a top for our furnace?" asked Chrys.

"We have bricks and a stovepipe, but what about the metal top?"

"There's more stovepipe than we need," said Ko-Ko. "If we take a piece of that and cut it and flatten it out, it would make a top for the furnace."

"That's a good idea," said Louly. "Can we use the garden shears to cut the stovepipe?"

"There are some metal cutters in the shed," said Ko-Ko.

"Why do you call it a furnace?" asked Vince. "Our furnace is a great big thing in the basement."

"Chrys doesn't even have a furnace in her grandma's house," said Poo-Bah.

"We call it a furnace because we like the name," said Louly. "It sounds more important than stove."

"And more romantical," said Cordy and Chrys.

By the time the furnace was finished and inspected by Chrys's grandmother, everyone was very hungry. Ko-Ko and Matt found wood and built the fire in the pit and Louly fried the bacon while Cordy and Chrys cut up many raw potatoes. Poo-Bah and Vince got tin plates and forks out of the camping kit and they all sat around expectantly.

It took the potatoes a long time to fry and some of them *were* rather raw as well as hard and brown, but there were enough to go around and they tasted good.

Aunt Eugenia arrived with a large plate of cookies and a pitcher of lemonade at a strategic moment when they had eaten all the raw fries they could bear and still felt a little hungry.

After lunch the boys disappeared to play baseball in the Larks' backyard.

"Now that we are rid of them," said Louly, "we can begin to organize our camp. We'll need some orange crates to store our food and dishes in, and a packing case for a table, and we'll have to bring out some old blankets and quilts to make up our beds in the tent."

There was certainly plenty to do, and the four girls busied themselves by hauling boxes out of the shed and setting up a neat and tidy camp around the furnace.

"We can wash our dishes at the faucet where the hose attaches, and store them away in the orange-crate cupboards, and housekeeping will be very easy," Louly promised.

"Good!" everybody cried.

"And, when we're all through working," Louly said, "if we are hot and tired, we'll put on our bathing suits and take a dip in the mountain spray."

"How in the world can we do that, Louly?" Poo-Bah cried.

Chrys and Cordy looked at Louly expectantly

too. Like a magician taking a rabbit out of a hat, Louly could always produce a miracle when it was needed.

"We'll play like the sprinkler is a waterfall in the mountains," Louly said. "It will be just as cool and refreshing."

It was a busy and exciting day and nobody had time to remember that Mr. and Mrs. Tucker were well on their long journey to Michigan and that Mrs. Tucker was probably still shedding large tears into her best handkerchief. Nobody remembered poor Mrs. Tucker, that is, until they went in the house to change into bathing suits. Then they suddenly thought of her because all of the things she usually did to make the house tidy had been left undone. The beds were not made, the breakfast dishes were not washed, and you could write your name in dust on the parlor table and the upright piano.

"Oh, dear!" said Louly. "I'm not being responsible!"

"But we were having fun," said Poo-Bah. "Let's not stop having fun."

"We won't," promised Louly, "but after we've had our dip in the mountain spray, I'll really have to do some housework."

"After our dip in the mountain spray, we'll have to work instead of play," said Chrys dreamily.

"Listen to Chrys," jeered Poo-Bah. "Shakespeare's a poet, and doesn't know it!"

"We'll help," offered Cordy. "It will be much more fun doing housework here than it would be at home."

"Indubitably!" agreed Chrys enthusiastically.

So after they had run shrieking through the sprinkler several times and got soaking wet, they came in and dried themselves, and began to clean up the Tuckers' house.

"Why do houses have to get dirty?" Poo-Bah wanted to know. "It's a nuisance!"

"We have to live in them," said Louly. "To keep them clean is like washing our own faces, or like paying rent for a nice place to live. Let's play like we're cleaning up the Crystal Palace."

"What is the Crystal Palace?" asked Poo-Bah. "Not Chrys's house, I guess?"

"It's something in England," Louly said. "I don't know just what, but it sounds very elegant, I think. So let's make it shine."

Louly and Cordy made up the beds, while Chrys and Poo-Bah did up the breakfast dishes. Then, while Louly pushed the carpet sweeper, the other girls dusted, and finally they wiped up the kitchen floor where they had tracked in water and wet grass.

"But Ko-Ko didn't mow or water the lawn," said Poo-Bah. "*He* ought to work too."

"I'll tell him when he comes in," promised Louly.

"We watered *part* of the lawn," said Chrys, remembering the soggy place where they had gone leaping and dancing through the sprinkler.

"Are we having raw fries again for supper?" Poo-Bah asked.

"No," said Louly slowly. "Once a day for those should be enough. Play like the forest ranger invited us for dinner in his mountain cabin tonight, and I'll cook scrambled eggs indoors and I'll make a salad, if you'll go out in the garden and get some lettuce and radishes and green onions."

"Grandma will let me bring a loaf of new-baked bread," Chrys said, "and maybe some more cookies."

"I can bring canned peaches," offered Cordy, "and pickles."

Louly stopped and looked at them. "Are you going to stay here all the time?" she asked.

"Well—" said Chrys.

"We just thought—in case you needed us," said Cordy.

"We're going to sleep out with you tonight," said Chrys.

"Aren't we?" asked Cordy.

"It's just that I'm trying to be responsible," Louly said. "You'll have to plan things with your families."

"Oh, please let them stay, Louly!" cried Poo-Bah. "Think how lonely we would be without them!"

"We're all camping together, aren't we?" said Cordy wistfully.

"Yes," Louly said, "and I like that, and you share the work and we all have fun, but you'll have to get permission. Chrys is right next door and can always ask, but I think Cordy better pack a bag and get her mother's permission to stay as long as the camping lasts. Let's all go over and ask Mrs. Lark right now."

Mrs. Lark looked doubtfully at the four eager faces.

"Louly, are you sure that you want to have all of these extra people in your family?"

"There are only two of them, Mrs. Lark," said Poo-Bah. Cordy and Chrys were silent. They didn't want to say anything to spoil their chances of being allowed to stay. If Cordy couldn't go camping at the Tuckers', Chrys's aunt was likely to withhold permission, too.

"It's all right," Louly said. "I really want to have them. They help a lot, and we are playing like we are camping out this week. I'm sure Mother wouldn't object."

"Mrs. Tucker asked us to look after them," said Cordy.

"And Aunt Eugenia and Grandma are next door in case of emergencies," offered Chrys.

"We thought," said Louly, "that you could just consider that you were sending Cordy to a mountain resort for a week of vacation, Mrs. Lark."

"Very well," Mrs. Lark said. "Pack a bag, Cordy, and I'll collect a basket of food to send over so you won't eat the Tuckers out of house and home."

Amid screams of delight they rushed off to help Cordy pack. Grandma and Aunt Eugenia had already been a part of the excitement of making camp, and it was not hard to persuade them that Chrys might stay for dinner at the Tuckers' too.

"We are having strawberry shortcake for dessert," Aunt said. "But I made an extra large one and I'll send over enough for all of you."

So they had a banquet, and after the supper dishes were done, Louly played the piano and they sang "Down by the Old Mill Stream" and "Oh, Susannah!" and "Carry Me Back to Old Virginny."

"Suffering cats!" exclaimed Ko-Ko on his way upstairs to bed. "I hope this doesn't go on all night."

"It won't," said Louly. "We're just waiting for the fall of darkness." It was one of the longest days of summer, but when it finally grew dark the girls undressed in Louly's room and put on their robes and slippers. Louly lighted the kerosene lantern that was part of the camping equipment, and led the way downstairs and out the back door.

The tent gleamed large and pale in the starlight. A cool breeze had come up to blow away the heat of the afternoon. Nobody said a word—it was almost scary. The three younger girls followed Louly's bobbing lantern in a ghostly procession across the grass to the entrance of the tent. They had already spread their blankets and comforters on the canvas floor and each camper knew which quarter of the space belonged to her. There was a fresh, dewy smell of crushed grass. When Louly took the lantern into the tent, the walls suddenly glowed a warm orange color, and the shadows of the girls inside the tent loomed large and queerly shaped, like moving figures in a magic-lantern show.

Chrys was the last one in the procession and before she ducked under the tent flap, she stood for a moment looking up at the sky. There seemed to be more stars in the sky than she had ever noticed before, and the Milky Way was like a far, mysterious river. Even her little sleeping porch had never seemed so much outdoors as this.

Cordy stuck her head out of the tent flap. "Hurry up, Chrys, if we don't put out the lantern, we'll have a flock of mosquitoes."

Chrys shivered a little and came in to creep silently into her blankets.

"Tell us a story, Louly," Cordy said when the lantern was extinguished.

"Not really a story," Louly said, "but listen! Imagine we're really out in the forest in the mountains. What do you hear?"

"I hear mosquitoes singing," said Cordy.

"Something more," said Louly in her play-like voice.

"I hear a cricket," said Poo-Bah.

"No, no," Louly said. "Listen harder! Don't you hear it? It's the mountain stream, falling over the cliff and rushing down the gorge."

"That's the breeze in the box-elder tree," said Cordy.

"Listen harder!" Louly said. "Use your imaginations. The stream is rushing down beside our tent. Can't you hear it? Can't you feel the cool, fresh spray?"

Chrys lay quite still, and goose flesh came out all over her. She felt the spray of the imaginary stream like tiny prickles of ice all up and down her spine.

It was even colder and fresher than the spray from the lawn sprinkler.

"Are there bears?" asked Poo-Bah.

"Certainly not," said Louly. "Billy is just outside the tent and this is a magic forest where nothing will hurt us. But sometimes, over the sound of the river, you can hear a hoot owl saying 'Who? Who?' He is the sentinel of the forest and he and Billy are guarding us. And in the morning we'll drop our lines in the river and catch a trout for breakfast."

"I'd rather have Shredded Wheat, Louly."

"All right," Louly said. "Go to sleep now, everybody. Last one asleep is a tardy turtle."

"Louly, do *you* know when you go to sleep? *I* don't."

"Nobody does," said Louly. "How could you?"

Silence descended on the tent in the magic forest.

Chrys lay awake thinking: "In the dark woods the mountain stream is falling. It rushes down, down, down, among the forest trees. The spray is like white horses leaping and bounding. Their manes and tails are gleaming in the starlight. They are going to join the river of the Milky Way."

She said it over to herself several times. It felt like a poem. "But it hasn't any rhymes or moral, so it can't be a poem," she thought. "Maybe tomorrow

I can put it into rhymes." But sometimes getting a good thought into the strait jacket of rhyme seemed to spoil the good thought and nothing worthwhile was left. She sighed and then she said her good thought about the river over again to herself. She was the last one in the tent to go to sleep, and she did not know when it happened.

4 · Letters

Chrys had been saving her allowance for several weeks to buy fireworks for the Fourth of July. The Fourth was an important day in Warsaw, Idaho, in 1908. Nearly everyone in town went to see the parade or else took part in it, and the parade was followed by the Pioneer Picnic in the park. You did not have to be a pioneer to attend the picnic. It was fun for young and old. There were three-legged races and jumping competitions, and a band concert and speeches and recitations. In the evening there were dancing parties and displays of fireworks all over town. From daybreak to dark, firecrackers could be heard popping and banging.

Chrystal's dog, Rowdy, had very sensitive ears and he was terrified of loud noises. He usually spent the day shivering and shaking, in the farthest, darkest corner under Grandma's bed. When Chrys knelt down and tried to coax him out, she could see his eyes shining in the dark. But although he trusted and loved and obeyed her every other day of the year, on the Fourth of July he would not come out from his dark corner.

This was the only part of the Fourth that Chrys did not like. She loved every other bit of it, and the best of all came in the evening when skyrockets and Roman candles shot colored balls of light into the darkness.

Chrystal's grandma always took charge of shooting off the fireworks on the hill on the evening of the Fourth. Although she did not go out to the parade or the Pioneer Picnic or listen to the band and the speeches, she was the mistress of ceremonies at the final glory of the evening. She saw to it that wooden troughs were made for shooting off the big rockets, and she made the children point the Roman candles away from houses or each other and hold them at arm's length while they waved them slowly back and forth. Before they were lighted, she saw that the pinwheels were securely nailed to tree trunks where they could do no damage. She was a benevolent tyrant. But the children did not mind, because she also made sure that each one had time to shoot off his own fireworks for everyone else to see. In this way the display lasted a long time and every person had his proper amount of admiration and appreciation. In some neighborhoods all of the fireworks were shot off at one time and sometimes children got burned and others felt that they were cheated or had not had their money's worth of fun.

Chrys's grandma enjoyed it as much as the children did. They sensed this, and also sensed that things went better when she made the rules. So in a state of great excitement, the neighborhood children gathered around the cement mounting block at the top of the hill in front of Chrys's house, waiting for the sky to become dark. When the last green glow had died out of the western sky and the first skyrocket had gone up from across town on College Hill, Grandma would say, "*Now!* One at a time. Who is first? Ko-Ko? Good. Everybody stand back and watch."

So that was why Chrys saved her money and put a lot of thought into what kind of fireworks she would purchase.

"Chrys," said Louly on the second day of camping, while they were washing the greasy raw-fries pan under the garden hose, "have you ever driven your pony cart in the Fourth of July parade?"

"No," Chrys said, "I never thought of it. Maybe Tommy would be scared of the firecrackers or the band. I don't know."

"Well, think about it," Louly said. "We could decorate the cart with flags and bunting, and make red, white, and blue rosettes for Tommy's bridle. We four girls could ride in the cart. It might be fun."

"Oh, swell," cried Cordy. "We could dress up some way in old-fashioned costumes or something."

"Nothing fancy," Louly said. "It should be tasteful and dignified. The decorations should go on the pony and cart, not on ourselves."

"But what would we be?" asked Poo-Bah. "They'll have a float with a Goddess of Liberty, and men in wigs to sign the Declaration of Independence, and maybe Indians—"

"We all have middy blouses," Louly said. "If we wore dark skirts and middies we would look very dignified and we could represent the Navy."

"Dear me!" said Chrys. "You've thought it all out,

haven't you? But would they *let* us be in the parade, just like that, without anybody inviting us?"

"Ko-Ko is going to play the trombone in the young men's marching band," Louly said, "and I told him to ask the band leader to ask the marshal of the parade to ask Mrs. Wendell, who is running the program, if it would be all right."

"Louly thinks of everything!" said Cordy admiringly. "Even who to ask to ask who."

"Louly, you ought to be speaking a piece on the afternoon program," said Chrys.

"Don't think that I couldn't!" said Louly proudly. She struck a dramatic attitude and cried out in a ringing voice:

" 'Shoot if you must this old gray head,
    But spare your country's flag,' she said."

"Oh, Louly," the girls cried. "Why don't you get Ko-Ko to ask the band leader to ask the marshal to ask Mrs. Wendell if you can speak a piece on the afternoon program?"

Louly laughed. "No," she said. "I'd really like to do it, but you just don't ask to do things like that. You just have to wait around and around until somebody asks you first. It's like getting invited to dance. You have to sit with the wallflowers until someone comes up and says, 'Miss Louisa Lee

Tucker, may I have the extreme honor of asking you to stand up with me and dance the next two-step?' And then I say, 'Why, thank yo' all so ve'y, ve'y much. Ah'd sho' nuff admiah to accept yo' cha'min offah, Suh!' "

"Oh, Louly!" they gasped, helpless with laughter, and then Poo-Bah said, "She's thinking of when Eddie Wendell asked her for a dance at the high school prom."

"I *am not!*" said Louly indignantly.

"Eddie Wendell!" cried Cordy. "Why, it's *his* mother—"

"No, I'm not going to speak a piece," said Louly positively.

One morning the postman brought the Tucker children a letter from Michigan. Everyone crowded around to hear Louly read it.

"My darling, darling children:

"Oh, how we miss you! I would come right home now if I could, but Grandma Lee is so ill. And she was so happy to see us. They say our being here has done her a world of good. I am able to relieve the nurse and help in taking care of her. Only a few weeks more now and I hope that she will be well enough for us to leave.

"I hope that there have been no emergencies, and that you are not too sad and lonesome."

"Have there been any emergencies?" asked Cordy.

"I can't think of any," Louly said.

"There's still time," said Poo-Bah hopefully.

"And you don't look sad and lonesome," Chrys said. "Have you been?"

"Well, just a little bit in spots and snatches," Louly said. "We've been too busy to think about it."

"Go on reading," Poo-Bah said.

"There isn't much more," said Louly. "She says, '*I have to go now, it is time for the doctor's visit. But do write to us, darling children. We worry about you every day and pray for you at night. Your very loving Mother.*' And here Daddy has written at the bottom, '*Chins up, kids,*' and he's made a lot of X's for kisses."

"What a sweet letter," said Chrystal wistfully. She thought, "How wonderful to have a mother and father to write a letter like that," but she didn't say what she thought. It was better to pretend that she was just like everybody else.

"Now, I s'pose, we'll have to take pen in hand and write an answer," Poo-Bah said.

"We certainly will," said Louly. "We'll all write,

even Chrys and Cordy. And we'll draw pictures of the tent and the furnace and tell about our plays— everything we can think of."

"That will be fun," said Chrys. "You're sure you don't mind having Cordy and me write too?"

"No, they'll love to hear from all of us. I'll put this mail for Daddy up on the desk in his study, and I'll bring down a lot of writing paper. We can all sit around the dining room table and write."

In a moment Louly was back distributing pencils and paper. "Play like we're getting out a newspaper," she said. "Each one of us can be a special reporter. We'll save sports and lawn-mowing for Ko-Ko to write, and we'll divide up the other departments between us."

"What other departments?"

"Well, society, theater, outdoor life—"

"We haven't had much society," objected Cordy, "but I could do the plays and plans for the Fourth of July."

"I think Louly should choose what *she* wants to write," said Chrys. "After all, they are her parents."

"Well, I'll tell about the camping out," said Louly. "That can be outdoor life, and, Chrys, how would you like to do household hints and recipes?"

"That's all right with me," said Chrys, "if you'll

let me tell about the baking-powder biscuits and raw fries."

Louly laughed. "All right," she said.

For the rest of the morning they were busy scribbling. Poo-Bah filled many pages with cartoons and comic strips. She laughed so much while she was doing it that the lines came out all crooked and wobbly.

"I think they look more funny-peculiar than funny-ha-ha," said Cordy, looking over Poo-Bah's shoulder.

"Anyway, I think they'll laugh," said Poo-Bah cheerfully.

Louly and Cordy wrote very neat and eloquent descriptions of what they had been doing, and Chrys wrote a poem.

> "Louly made some biscuits,
> She thought they would be good
> But without baking powder
> They tasted more like wood.
> But then she made some raw fries
> Outdoors in a pan
> And now we think they are the best
> Kind of food for man.
> This ends my poem of household hints,
> I haven't written any since."

When the letters were finished, they took them to Aunt Eugenia.

"Please, Miss Eugenia," said Louly, "will you write that there have been no emergencies? It will make my parents feel happier to hear it from you."

Aunt Eugenia wrote: *"The children are getting along beautifully. There have been no emergencies and they are having a good time. Feel free to stay as long as you are needed. Affectionately, Eugenia."*

"And now Billy," said Louly.

"You don't mean to say that Billy has to write a letter?" cried Poo-Bah.

"Why, certainly," said Louly. "We'll dip his paw in ink and set it down on a piece of paper. It will be his signature."

It was a fat letter when Ko-Ko had added his bit and it was all folded into a large envelope.

"But it will make them happy," Louly said.

5 · Fourth of July Parade

When Ko-Ko came home that afternoon he had good news.

"They'd like to have you in the parade," he said. "It's not as long as usual, and they are glad enough to get any lame ducks to march along. 'A pony cart?' they said. 'That will be dandy!' But you'll have to be at the south end of Main Street at nine-thirty sharp, and you'll have to be able to keep your horse under control with all of the bands and firecrackers and everything."

"Well," said Chrys, "I guess I can do it. At this time of year Tommy is very fat and lazy. The hardest thing is to make him go at all. In the spring it is quite different."

"I'll say it is!" said Cordy, remembering the early spring day when she and Chrys had ridden out to her father's farm on the Ridge and their horses had run away from them.

"Tommy will be fine," said Louly confidently. Louly had never driven a horse herself.

So some of the money that they might have spent on fireworks was laid out for red, white, and blue bunting and ribbon to make into rosettes for Tommy's bridle.

The flags that were stored in attics for most of the year were brought down to decorate the houses, and Chrys kept the nice, silk, middle-sized flag to stick up in the whip socket of the pony cart instead of the whip. The girls washed and ironed their white middy blouses and brushed and pressed their navy-blue skirts. They hosed off the pony cart and polished it until it shone. It was a two-wheel cart with a place for the driver and one passenger to sit facing the front. The other two passengers sat back-to-back with the front-seaters and looked in the opposite direction. Anyone who got seasick riding backward had better stay out of the pony cart. It had a very sea-going motion when the pony trotted.

Fortunately Chrys's pony did not often care to trot. In midsummer heat, he only worked himself up to a trot when he knew that he was on his way home to a cool, pleasant barn and a manger full of hay.

Tommy was fat, and that was because he loved to eat. He not only liked hay and oats, but juicy red apples and pea pods and candy—candy most of all. Peanut brittle was his favorite, and he had learned where the candy store and ice-cream parlor was located. If Chrys did not stop at the ice-cream parlor when they were jogging down Main Street, Tommy would turn in all by himself and wait there until somebody went in and bought him a small, striped bag of peanut brittle. Chrys was so pleased to know that he would do this all by himself that she rarely failed to buy him his reward. It took quite a lot of her allowance money, but she felt that it was worth it. Besides, she liked peanut brittle, too, and they usually shared the bag.

In preparation for the patriotic parade, Chrys brushed and curried Tommy and sponged him off to make his sorrel coat shine.

Everybody had a hand in preparing the lunch that they would take to the Pioneer Picnic. Aunt Eugenia made chicken salad and fresh rolls and Mrs. Lark made pies and a huge chocolate cake. Louly boiled two dozen eggs and deviled them according to her mother's best recipe.

"Don't leave anything out, Louly," everybody warned.

"Please, pul-*lease!*" said Louly. "I'll never leave out anything again, and these are going to be the best deviled eggs you ever tasted."

The young Larks and Tuckers and Chrys planned to have a table all to themselves under the trees in the park after the parade.

At the first streak of dawn on the Fourth, Ko-Ko set off a giant firecracker near the tent, and the four girls sprang out of their sleep with yelps of terror. Rowdy and Billy crawled under the beds in their respective houses, and the glorious day began.

By nine o'clock Ko-Ko, in a white shirt with a loop of red, white, and blue bunting over his shoulder, had departed with his trombone to join the band. The girls in their clean white middy blouses climbed into the shining cart with its patriotic decorations; Tommy tossed his rosetted head and began to trot down Third Street to South Main.

At the last moment Louly suddenly had second thoughts.

"Of course this is all pretty childish," she said. "I hope that no one I know sees me riding in a pony cart in a parade."

"Everybody in town will see you, of course," said Cordy sensibly. "That's what a parade is for. They'll be lining the sidewalks and hanging out of the windows."

"It's just that I'm probably too grown up to be doing this," Louly said, adding as a pleasant afterthought, "too *responsible*."

"She means she hopes that Eddie Wendell doesn't see her," Poo-Bah said.

"I did not mean any such thing, Paula Belle," said Louly indignantly. "Besides, Eddie Wendell is out of town for the summer."

"Then I don't think it's very nice of you to be ashamed to ride in Chrys's pony cart," Poo-Bah said. "You might make Chrys feel bad."

"That's all right," Chrys said. "I don't feel bad, and anyone who doesn't want to ride in the pony cart in the parade can get out and walk."

"It was your idea in the first place, Louly," said Cordy.

"Oh, for goodness' sake!" cried Louly. "I didn't

mean anything unpleasant. I'm having a wonderful time—it's all part of our having fun. Aren't you all having fun?"

"Indubitably!" the others shouted.

The Grand Marshal of the parade looked them over with approval.

"Very nice!" he said. "Better than I thought you'd be. The Navy, eh? That's a nice, patriotic idea. How would you like to head up the second section of the parade? Just before the Liberty float and the marching band?"

"That would be swell," said Poo-Bah.

"Swellissimus!" corrected Cordy.

"Ah da'e say we'd admiah to do that," murmured Louly in her Southern accent.

"It will be all right," agreed Chrys, "if the pony behaves himself. I've never driven him in a parade before."

"Horses are always unpredictable," the Grand Marshal said, "but a nice little fat pony like this is a better bet than some of the big, lively ones. Get in line there. You'll do just fine."

Promptly at ten the first section of the parade started to move. The Mayor rode in an open carriage with three pretty girls who tossed out roses and leaflets telling about the program at the Pioneer Picnic. Then the old soldiers limped along carrying flags, and the fife and drum corps played. Most of the merchants had floats advertising their businesses and the Ladies of the Rebecca Lodge marched in line carrying a garland of daisies. Finally it was time for Tommy to lead off the second section of the parade. At first he did not want to move and Chrys had no whip to threaten him. Tommy had never really been whipped, but when the whip came out of the socket and was flourished in the air, he knew it was the signal to trot. Today a flag in the whip socket was more beautiful than a whip, but not as useful. No whip was needed, however, when the young men's marching band struck up "Yankee Doodle." The drum boomed, the cymbals clashed, and Ko-Ko's trombone sounded *oom-pah-pah*!

Tommy gave a shake and a shudder and then started to trot briskly down the street. Chrys held a tight rein and in a moment the pony's trot slowed to a parade-sized walk. The girls began to wave and smile at the crowds of people standing along the sidewalk. Everything was going to be fine and dandy. A ripple of applause followed them as they rode along. Even Louly was perfectly happy now. She nodded and smiled, and didn't even reprove Poo-Bah for throwing kisses.

They proceeded for six or seven blocks in this delightful way, and now they were almost in the center of town. Just ahead of them was the chief hotel, and its front steps were crowded with people.

Suddenly Louly drew in her breath with a sharp hiss.

"Oh, there he is!" she said. "There's Eddie Wendell—himself! He's on the hotel steps. He's looking at *us*. Oh, don't look now, please!"

Of course all three girls looked. Eddie Wendell fluttered the hearts of all the girls in town—even the hearts of little ones like Poo-Bah. He was the best-looking boy in the senior class at high school and the best quarterback on the football team, and he lived in one of the biggest houses on the biggest hill, and his mother was the town arranger. The three younger girls had never exchanged a word with him, but at the commencement in May, Louly had danced three dances with Eddie Wendell. Ever since that time she turned quite pink whenever his name was mentioned. She turned pink now, and said, "I thought he was going to be away for the summer. I never thought . . . he'd see me riding in a pony cart like this. . . . Oh, dear!"

"It's a perfectly good pony cart," said Cordy staunchly. "Why shouldn't you be riding in it?"

"It looks so—so juvenile," said Louly unhappily.

As they passed the hotel steps, a cheer went up.

"Hooray for the Navy!" someone shouted, and "Hi, Louisa Lee Tucker!" cried Eddie Wendell, waving both hands at them. "Hi, Louly!"

"He was pleased to see you, Louly," Poo-Bah said.

"Oh, dear!" said Louly.

Tommy went jogging on by and the crowd of spectators on the hotel steps was left behind them. Tommy had behaved very well so far. Chrys kept a firm rein and even the occasional popping of a fire-cracker had not disturbed him. He tossed his head and lifted his feet as if he had been born to the circus and as if parades were everyday events in his career. But in the block after the hotel came the ice-cream parlor. No one had thought to worry about that. Who could imagine that a pony in a parade would remember where the peanut brittle was?

But there, with the band playing and the wheels turning and the people marching and all of the other people in town lining the sidewalks to watch, Tommy suddenly turned out of the procession and headed for Childers'.

Chrys jerked the reins and tried to turn him. She shouted at him, but he paid no attention to her. The front part of the parade went blithely on, but the second section behind the pony cart paused with a jolt. The Goddess of Liberty nearly fell off her stand, and the young men's marching band was thrown into confusion.

Tommy headed for the curb in front of the ice-cream parlor and stopped expectantly. Again Chrys reached for the whip, but it was not there. Could a patriotic person prod a balky pony with the Stars and Stripes?

"Oh, what shall I do? What shall I do?" cried Chrys. "I can't go in *now*, in the middle of a parade, and buy him a bag of candy!"

"It looks like you'll have to," Cordy said.

"It's terribly embarrassing," Louly muttered. "Make him go, Chrys. Can't you make him go?"

The band was *oom-pah-pah*ing right behind them. The whole second section of the parade had come to a halt and people up and down the street were shouting "What's the matter? What's the matter?"

"Oh, dear," wailed Chrys, "I didn't bring my purse. What are we going to do?"

"You'll have to get out and lead him," Poo-Bah said.

"Here, take the reins, Louly," cried Chrys. "It's the only thing to do. I'll have to get out and lead him."

But just then, elbowing his way through the

crowd, came a very romantical rescuer. How he got there so soon nobody knew, but Eddie Wendell had seen their predicament and had run all the way down the block with his best ball-carrying speed. Now he grasped Tommy's bridle and turned him back into the mainstream of the parade. The pony tossed his head and snorted, but the hand on his bridle was firm.

The band burst into "Stars and Stripes Forever," and everything began to move again. *Oom-pah-pah, oom-pah-pah!*

Eddie led the pony until they were safely past Childers', then he dropped the bridle and walked along beside them for a moment.

"I always did want to join the Navy," he said, looking into Louly's eyes.

"Ah was nevah so humiliated in all mah bo'n days," said Louly in her Southern accent.

"Listen! Don't go away at the end of the parade. I'll see you there. Remember?"

"Ah'll remembah," Louly said. Now she was beginning to smile again.

Eddie dropped back into the crowd; the parade went on in a wave of applause.

"Isn't he wonderful?" murmured Cordy.

"He surely saved us from a dreadful fate," said Chrys.

"He must have liked us pretty much," said Poo-Bah.

"What do you think he'll say to us at the end of the parade?" wondered Cordy.

"Maybe he'll ask us all to have ice-cream sodas with him," suggested Chrys.

"This time, I think I'll try mixing pineapple with chocolate," said Poo-Bah.

"He's the dreamiest, creamiest waltzer," Louly said in a hushed voice, "but I sho' nuff thought he was out of town."

6 · Louly Is a Dastard

A lot of people were milling around at the end of the parade.

"He probably won't be here anyway," Louly said. "Why should he be?" But there he was!

Poo-Bah stood up in the cart and waved and shouted. "Here *we* are!" she said.

The younger girls were already imagining how

the ice-cream sodas were going to taste after a long, hot parade.

Eddie came over and stood beside them, but he looked only at Louly.

"You were real good to help us out," Chrys said. "Thank you!"

"The pony always stops at the ice-cream parlor," Poo-Bah said. "He likes peanut brittle. We do, too, but we like ice-cream sodas even better, don't we?"

"Indubitably," said Cordy.

"I thought you we'e gone fo' the summah, Eddie," Louly said in a quiet voice.

"I'm just back for the Fourth, Louly," said Eddie, "just two days. Will you come and have lunch with us at the picnic, Louly? My mother's having a party for us."

"Oh, I couldn't . . . ," Louly said. "I just don't think I could. Your mother wouldn't want an extra—"

"Yes, she would. My mother wants to see you anyway, Louly. You give recitations, don't you? My mother's in charge of the program this afternoon, and one of the speakers failed her. I told her I'd see if I could get you—"

"Oh, I couldn't," Louly faltered.

"She knows 'Shoot if you must this old gray head,' " said Poo-Bah.

"That would be fine, Louly," said Eddie. "Come on. Do!"

"But she can't go for lunch," continued Poo-Bah, "because she's eating lunch with us, and she made all the deviled eggs and everything."

Louly drew a long breath. "Suppose you let me speak fo' myse'f, kidlet," she said to Poo-Bah. She gave Eddie her hand and stepped out of the pony cart with the grace and dignity of a queen.

"I should be most happy to have lunch with yo' pa'ty, Eddie," Louly said, "and you may tell yo' mothah that I can always give a recitation if eme'gency demands it."

The three girls in the cart stared at Louly in speechless wonder.

"But you were eating with *us*," said Cordy.

"She's coming with me now, aren't you, Louly?" said Eddie eagerly. "My horse and buggy are tied up just around the corner. My folks will be real pleased."

Louly hesitated for just an instant. Then she said in her best grown-up, play-acting voice, "Run along now, chillun, and be good. Ah'll see yo' all latah."

There was nothing to do but drive off. Louly strolled away with Eddie toward his horse and buggy.

"Traitor!" hissed Cordy.

"I never saw her act like that before," said Poo-Bah. "Wait till I tell Ko-Ko. He'll be mad as hops."

"If that's what she calls being responsible!" said Cordy.

"Well," said Chrys, "you can see she likes him a lot. But I think it was really the recitation part that got her. She loves to speak pieces, and here was a chance. You can hardly blame her. Still and all. . . ."

"It's treason!" said Cordy.

"Just you wait till Ko-Ko hears!" threatened Poo-Bah.

"Well—" said Chrys unhappily, "she *did* desert us."

The magic of the day had gone. They jogged on home and put the pony in the barn. Aunt Eugenia had the picnic baskets packed for them and the park was not far away.

"Where's Louly?" everyone wanted to know.

"She's eating with the Wendells."

"The Wendells? Why ever the Wendells?"

"That Eddie asked her. She's going to speak a piece on the program."

"How *nice!*" cried Aunt Eugenia. "I'm so happy for Louly."

"We aren't," said Poo-Bah. "We think that she's a deserter and a traitor and—what else?"

"Deserter and traitor, that's enough, isn't it?" said Cordy, but Chrys said: "Dastard!"

"Yes, she's a dastard," the other two agreed. Nobody really knew what a dastard was, but it sounded exactly right to describe Louly's behavior.

Lunch was not half so much fun without Louly, and yet everyone had to admit that her deviled eggs were delicious. They ate them all up, and Poo-Bah said with satisfaction, "Well, at least she'll never know how good they tasted—that's something."

"Do you s'pose she's still talking with a Southern accent?" wondered Chrys. "I should think it would be hard to keep it up."

"She's pretty good at it," Poo-Bah said. "She can go on for quite a long time."

When the program started, the crowd of picnickers gathered around the bandstand to watch and listen. There were benches for the older people, and the children sat on the grass or chased each other around at the edge of the crowd.

Chrys and Cordy and Poo-Bah were not able to get very close to the bandstand, but they found a place to sit where they could see and hear. A girls' chorus sang "The Star-Spangled Banner" and the Mayor made a long and tiresome speech. A boy in spectacles with a red necktie recited the Declaration of Independence, and another boy with spectacles and a blue necktie recited Lincoln's Gettysburg Address. Poo-Bah lay back on the grass and was going to sleep, when both Cordy and Chrys began to prod her.

"Poo-Bah! Sit up. She's coming next. It's Louly!"

Poo-Bah sat up with a start. All of the other dozers on a hot, tiresome afternoon sat up too. It was as if a breeze of expectation had stirred the leaves of the trees.

Louly stood out alone on the steps of the bandstand. She looked pale but composed. She smoothed down her middy blouse and shook back her hair. She seemed very far away to the three girls who were watching her, as if they were seeing her through the large end of a telescope.

"Oh, Louly, don't forget," murmured Chrys under her breath. She could only think how terrified she herself would be if she found herself in Louly's shoes. She would forget everything, *everything* she had known!

But now Louly's voice came firm and strong.

"Good afternoon, ladies and gentlemen," she said. "I am now going to recite for you a poem called 'Barbara Frietchie' by John Greenleaf Whittier."

"She's lost it!" said Poo-Bah.

"What? What has she lost?"

"The Southern accent."

"Ssh!"

There was a moment of expectant silence. Everyone was awake and listening now for the familiar story of Stonewall Jackson's encounter with the brave old woman of Frederick town.

Louly's voice was quiet as she started the poem, but everybody heard it.

> *"Up from the meadows rich with corn,*
> *Cool in the clear September morn,*
> *The clustered spires of Frederick stand*
> *Green-walled by the hills of Maryland."*

Chrys could feel her hair begin to prickle on the top of her head. Little icy shivers ran down her spine, as when Louly made them imagine a mountain river.

The poetry flowed on quietly—

> *"Forty flags with their silver stars,*
> *Forty flags with their crimson bars,*
> *Flapped in the morning wind: the sun*
> *Of noon looked down, and saw not one."*

But now Louly's quiet voice rose and grew brisk as if on the wings of a mounting breeze. Now the audience began to see Barbara Frietchie as she took one of the flags that had been hauled down by the rebels and unfurled it defiantly from her attic window. They could hear the marching feet of the invading soldiers as Louly's voice marched in cadence. When she cried *"Halt!"* and *"Fire!"* everyone was there with her in mounting breathlessness. Her voice rang out in triumph on the familiar "Shoot if you must this old gray head!" line, and again on Stonewall Jackson's command to his soldiers.

> " *'Who touches a hair of yon gray head*
> *Dies like a dog! March on!' he said."*

After that Louly's voice grew gradually quieter, as if the tramp of soldiers' feet were receding into the distance. The last two lines were spoken very softly, but everybody heard them.

> *"And ever the stars above look down*
> *On thy stars below in Frederick town!"*

Then the audience was clapping and Louly made a bow and then she went away.

The girls tried to reach her, but there were so many people in between that they finally had to give it up.

"Well, she did it!" said Poo-Bah. "Didn't she?"

"Yes, she did!"

"She was wonderful!"

They all loved Louly once again and were very proud of her, but there was no opportunity to tell her so. The program went on, and Louly had vanished somewhere with the Wendells.

"We'll tell her how good she was, after we get home and before the fireworks," the girls said to each other.

But they were delayed in getting home, the sun was almost down, and when they reached the Tuckers' house, Louly was not there. They raised the tent flap and the tent was empty. Ko-Ko came to join them, and he didn't know where Louly was either.

"She has vanished off the face of the earth," said Chrys solemnly in one of the grandiose phrases that she enjoyed using.

"She's run out on us again," said Cordy more practically.

"Are you looking for Louly?" asked Aunt Eugenia, coming out on the side porch to wave at them.

"Yes. Do you know where she is?"

"She just left a few minutes ago," Aunt Eugenia said. "I gave her permission. The Wendells are having a dancing party on their lawn tonight, and Mrs. Wendell called me to see if it was all right. Louly dashed in to change into her best dress. She looked real pretty. You would have been proud of her."

"She went off and deserted us again," said Poo-Bah darkly. "She's a deserter."

"She's a traitor and a—"

"A dastard!" supplied Chrys angrily.

"Why, girls," said Aunt Eugenia, "I'm amazed to hear you talk like that. Mrs. Wendell said that Louly made a perfectly marvelous recitation—the best thing on the program."

"It was tolerable," said Cordy.

"There were lots of other good things on the program," said Chrys.

"Mama wouldn't have wanted her to go away and leave us," Poo-Bah said.

"On the contrary," Aunt Eugenia said, "I think your mother would have been very pleased. Louly's growing up, and she ought to have older company. It's just because she's so nice and good-natured that she spends so much time with you younger girls."

"Kidlets, you mean," said Chrys.

"Chillun," added Cordy sourly.

"Well, you're all tired and cross," said Aunt Eugenia. "Come in now and get some bread and milk and rest a few minutes before the fireworks start. It's going to be an exciting evening."

It was an exciting evening in spite of not having Louly with them. In the blaze of rockets, blooming like gigantic colored flowers from all the hilltops of town, the three younger girls could almost forgive and forget that Louly had deserted them.

But when the fireworks were over, and the dogs timidly emerged from under the beds, and the lights began to go out in the houses, music still sounded on the hill where the Wendells lived, and Louly had not come home.

Even Ko-Ko began to be worried. "I'll go over to the Wendells' and see if she needs me to walk her home," he said.

"I expect that Eddie will walk her home," said Poo-Bah.

"Well, I'll see, anyhow. You girls get to bed. There's no use waiting up."

Silently Chrys and Cordy and Poo-Bah undressed in Louly's room. They could see what a hurry she had been in when she changed her clothes for the party. Her blue serge skirt was flung over the back of a chair and her middy blouse was in a heap on the floor. A wet towel was draped over the side of the bathtub and talcum powder was spilled on the rug.

"Aunt Eugenia said she looked very nice," said Chrys wistfully.

"I should think she would be tired by now," said Cordy. "We all got up so early."

"She's never tired when she can dance," said Poo-Bah.

"Let's not speak to her in the morning," said Cordy.

"I won't speak to her," said Poo-Bah, "not ever again, if I live to be a hundred years."

"Oh, yes you will, Poo-Bah," said Chrys. "You're her sister. There will be Christmases and family reunions and things. Maybe she'll even marry Eddie Wendell and you'll have to be a bridesmaid or carry her train or something."

"No, never," said Poo-Bah, yawning and rubbing her eyes.

They lit the lantern and filed out to the tent. Chrys couldn't help thinking that her own bed would have been more comfortable than a heap of blankets on the canvas floor of the tent. Without Louly there was not much magic in camping, and they were all dead tired.

Poo-Bah went to sleep as soon as she crawled into her blankets, but rockets were still bursting in the dark when Chrys closed her eyes.

After a while Cordy whispered, "Are you asleep, Chrys?"

"No."

"Do you think we've lost her?"

"Indubitably," Chrys said, "but who cares?"

"That's right," said Cordy, "who cares?"

After that they were silent; but they did care. Louly was a deserter and a traitor and a dastard, and they never wanted to speak to her again, but still. . . .

7 · The Marvelous Fifth

In the morning Chrys awoke to a pleasant and familiar smell. It was a smell of dewy grass and sweet peas and damp blankets, and something else, something that made her mouth water. There was a sound, too, a sound of sizzling like the sizzling of bacon and raw fries in a frying pan. Bacon and raw fries! That accounted for the delicious smell.

Chrys sat up in bed and looked around her. The sun was hot on one side of the tent and it lit up the interior like a bright lamp.

"I overslept," Chrys thought. "Cordy must be getting breakfast."

But when she looked at Cordy's bed, she saw Cordy's tousled head among the blankets. Cordy was peacefully asleep, and beyond her lay Poo-Bah, still lost to the world.

Chrys's heart began to harden. Someone was cooking breakfast. It must be Louly. What was she going to say to her? Or wasn't she going to speak to her at all? Chrys got up slowly and put on her robe and slippers. She opened the tent flap and looked out.

Louly, in an old calico apron, was leaning over the furnace. Her face was flushed and smiling. Under her breath she was humming a little tune.

"Well, Cinderella," said Chrys coldly, "how was the ball?" Chrys meant to sound sarcastic, but a little genuine curiosity must have seeped through, for Louly looked up with shining eyes. "Oh, it was wonderful!" she said. "They had Japanese lanterns lighted and hanging in the trees, and they had this real swell dancing floor and someone to play the piano and a violin and a flute. And, oh, the food, Chrys! It was yummy, and I danced every dance, Chrys, every one."

"Didn't you get tired?" asked Chrys, reluctantly finding herself involved in a conversation with a dastard. She came and sat on a box beside the furnace, and Louly gave her a tin plate full of bacon and raw fries.

"Oh, no," said Louly, filling her own plate, "not while I was dancing. Oh, it was heavenly, and we could see the skyrockets going off all over town on the other hills."

"Did you dance all the dances with Eddie?"

"Of course not! They had all sorts of other people there, and when Ko-Ko came for me, they made him stay, and even Ko-Ko danced! Can you imagine that? Ko-Ko dancing!"

Chrys couldn't help laughing because they knew so well how Ko-Ko disdained girls and parties and all of the finer social graces. At least he said he did.

Cordy and Poo-Bah stuck their heads out of the tent flap.

"Why are you laughing?"

"I thought we weren't going to speak to her ever again."

"You can speak to her now," said Chrys. "She's got a lot to tell."

"Get your plates, kids," said Louly, "the bacon and raw fries are ready to eat."

"We haven't washed our faces," objected Cordy.

"Never mind," Louly said, "—just this once. Tomorrow we'll start washing before breakfast and doing all the responsible things."

"Oh, let's not," said Poo-Bah.

"Yes, tomorrow," Louly said, "but today—today is a very special day."

"It is? What kind of a special day?"

"It's the Fifth of July," said Louly. "Didn't you ever hear about the Marvelous Fifth of July?"

"We've heard about the Glorious Fourth, but not about the Marvelous Fifth. What do we do?"

"It's the day we get over the Glorious Fourth, so all rules are off and we simply enjoy ourselves."

"Louly," said Poo-Bah, "we are very mad at you, so how can we enjoy ourselves?"

"It was probably bad of me to go off with the Wendells," Louly said. "I don't blame you for being mad, but I had such a dreamy, creamy time. It was right out of the fairy-tale book. And I gave a public recitation too. Did you hear that? Was it all right?"

"It was tolerable," said Cordy.

"No, it was better than that," said Chrys. "It was good. And we got along all right without you, even if we were mad."

"How were the deviled eggs?"

"Tolerable."

"Good."

"We ate them all up."

"Tell about the party, Louly," Chrys said, "and how even Ko-Ko danced."

So there they sat for nearly an hour, still in their night clothes and not even properly washed, while Louly recalled all the glories of the Wendells' dancing party. To hear Louly tell it was almost as good as being there in person.

"And did you use your Southern accent all the time, Louly?" asked Poo-Bah.

"My Southern accent?" repeated Louly. "Oh, I don't think so. I forget when I stopped using it. I was having such a good time."

"And what about Eddie Wendell?" Chrys asked. "I s'pose he'll be over here today, and you'll call us 'chillun' again."

"No, Eddie's working over in his uncle's store at Springdale this summer. But it's only twenty miles away, and do you know what?"

"What?"

"He's asked me to write to him. Think of that!"

"Oh, goody!" said Poo-Bah. "Maybe we can all write him a newspaper letter like the one we wrote Mother and Daddy."

"You don't understand these things, Poo-Bah," explained Chrys. "Eddie wants to hear from Louly. He doesn't want a newspaper."

"Well, then he doesn't know what he's missing," Poo-Bah said. "I could draw him some lovely funnies."

"So I expect you'll be sitting down to write Eddie a letter this morning, right in the middle of the Marvelous Fifth," complained Cordy.

"No," Louly said, "I'll wait for a responsible day to do my writing. Today I thought we'd start a new play. I woke up thinking about it this morning."

"Cinderella at the ball, I'll bet!" said Chrys.

"No, it's not a fairy tale this time. I thought I would play like I'm a very prim and proper young lady teacher who is sent into the back-country to teach the hillbillies, and you—"

"We know," cried Cordy, "we'll have to be the hillbillies!"

"But I thought it would be fun," said Louly. "You can all play tricks on me and do and say funny things, and I'll be very scandalized."

"I see possibilities," said Chrys.

"I even thought of our names," said Louly. "I would be Miss Permeliar Silverbottom, and I would be very rich, really, but very inexperienced; and you could be Seedy, Snoot, and Porky Rattletrap, and you would be poor but full of funny tricks."

"I speak to be Porky Rattletrap," shouted Poo-Bah.

"Well," Cordy said, "I wouldn't mind being Seedy."

"All right," said Chrys, "then I'll be Snoot."

"So now, instead of getting dressed in your regular clothes," said Louly, "go and look for all the funny old hillbilly-looking clothes you can find to put on, and I'll dress up in one of Mother's long dresses and a hat with a plume, and I'll try to teach you to spell and figure. You know the old blackboard that's up in the attic? And the funny old schoolbooks that Daddy saved because they were all wrong for modern teaching? We'll get out those, and we'll have a lot of fun with them."

So the Marvelous Fifth was a good day after all; and the anger at being called "chillun" and "kidlets" and being jealous of the Wendells and all the rest of it gradually wore away until it was forgotten.

Miss Silverbottom was very prim and exacting and the hillbillies thought of outrageous ways to thwart and tease her.

"Spell Mississippi, Porky."

"Miss-s-s-s-s-i."

"You forgot the *p*'s, Porky."

"Mip-p-p-p-i, Miss Silverbottom."

"No, no, that's not right either. You must mind your *p*'s and *q*'s."

"M-i-s-i-q-q-q-q-q-i."

"No, there's always a *u* after a *q*."

"M-u-s-s-s-q-u-s-p-p-i."

"How can you be so stupid?"

"It's very easy. You just stoop and start to skid, and then you're stoop-id."

"Oh, dear! What shall I do?"

"Give us a holiday to rest our brains."

"But you haven't any brains."

"We have pains and trains."

"That's not the same thing."

"Then if that's not the same thing, it must be something else."

"Elsa Puddleheimer, that's my great-grand-mother."

"Attention! Attention! Seedy, sit up straight. If you don't behave yourselves I'll rap your fingers with a ruler."

"I'd rather have you wrap them in a handker-chief."

"Oh, you are impossible!"

"Impassable! Impassable! Then we won't have to go to school any more."

It was very silly, but they laughed so hard that Aunt Eugenia ran out on the side porch to see what was the matter.

"My, you children look dreadful," she said. "Where in the world did you get those awful clothes?"

"This is one of Mr. Tucker's old shirts," said Cordy proudly. She had braided her hair into two little pigtails and tied each one with a piece of shoestring.

Poo-Bah was wearing a long-outgrown pair of Ko-Ko's knickers, and Chrys had on a torn nightshirt of Mr. Tucker's that had come out of the rag bag. Around the middle of it she had tied a blue sash, and her hair was combed straight up and pinned in a knot on the top of her head. Only Louly looked very beautiful and elegant.

The game went on for most of the day until finally Louly collapsed in the hammock under the crab-apple trees in Chrys's front yard. Her plumed hat lay on the grass, and her long skirt trailed in the dust in the worn place under the hammock.

"Go in and see what time it is," she said, "and get me a drink of water while I think what to do next."

The riotous hillbillies trooped away.

"Listen," Poo-Bah said, "I know where Ko-Ko keeps his trick glass. When you start to take a drink out of it, it dribbles water all over your front. That will be lovely for Miss Permeliar Silverbottom."

"Oh, swell!" said Chrys.

"Swellissimus!" said Cordy.

It took them quite a long time to find the trick glass, and then they had to carry it very carefully so as not to spill the water before the trick was accomplished. They returned in a solemn procession with their eyes fixed on the glass. Nobody noticed until they were quite close that Miss Permeliar Silverbottom was sound asleep in Chrys's hammock.

The hillbillies stood around and looked at her.

"Should we wake her?" they wondered.

"It's Sleeping Beauty herself," said Chrys in a hushed voice.

"No, it's Cinderella *after* the ball," said Cordy sensibly.

"I guess she's tired," said Poo-Bah.

"We could trickle a little of the water on her nose or down her neck. . . ."

"We *could*, but it would be sort of too bad. After all, she thought up the game."

"And it was a good one."

"We aren't really mad at her any more, are we?"

"No."

Very silently the hillbillies turned around and stole away. Chrys emptied the water out of the glass, and they went back to the Tuckers' house to change their clothes.

"Listen, kids," said Poo-Bah, "do you know how to make fudge?"

"Indubitably!" cried Cordy and Chrys together.

8 · The "Elktown Bugle"

Every Sunday morning before church a large Sunday paper was delivered on the front porch of Chrys's grandma's house. This was not a local paper, it came from the big city ninety miles away. Sometime in the night it was put on a train that brought it into Warsaw very early in the morning so that it could be delivered in the city. Nearly everybody in Warsaw took the *Elktown Bugle,* because it gave so much more world news than the *Warsaw Gazette*. It had a homemaker's section *and* the funny papers!

As soon as the children in the town heard the thud of the *Elktown Bugle* on their front porches they rushed out and grabbed the funny papers to read before Sunday School. There were the "Katzen-jammer Kids" and "Buster Brown" and "Little Nemo" and "The Dreams of the Rarebit Fiend," and all the other gaily colored cartoon pictures that everybody loved.

On the Saturday night after the Fourth of July the campers had gone to their own homes so that they could take Saturday-night baths and wash their hair and trim their fingernails and get a good sleep in a comfortable bed to make them decent for Sunday School. They planned to return to the tent by Louly's mountain stream on Sunday night when their best clothes were put away for another week.

So Chrys was all alone on her own front porch when she unfolded the *Elktown Bugle* on that July Sunday. She skimmed hastily over the funnies, chuckling softly to herself. Later in the afternoon she would read them over again, taking more time and savoring each one individually. As she finished each sheet of the paper she folded it neatly again so that Grandma wouldn't find it in a mess.

Grandma liked to have a tidy paper to read when she got around to it later in the day.

After the funnies, Chrys opened the homemaker's section to look at the Children's Page. She kept telling herself that she was too old for the Children's Page, but it was like telling herself that Louly was a dastard when all the while she could not help loving her.

There were puzzles and jokes and stories on the Children's Page, and drawings of animals and instructions for feeding pets or for making windmills and potholders and bookmarks. Anyway, it was always fun to read the Children's Page and see what new ideas it might contain.

This time it looked a little different. In the center of the page, instead of a drawing of clouds and trees in which were hidden cats and dogs and the faces of people, there was a blank space framed by solid lines. Underneath it said, "Next Sunday in this space we will print an original poem by one of our own young readers. Send your poem with your name and age to Aunt Augusta, in care of the Children's Page, *Elktown Bugle*, if you wish to see yourself in print."

Chrys sat for a moment, stunned by dazzling possibilities. To see one of her poems in print, in neat black letters as in a book! To have it in a news-

paper, and delivered with a thud on hundreds of
front porches on a Sunday morning! To be a pub-
lished author! But, of course, they would never take
one of *her* poems, the poem of a girl (a "kidlet,"
"one of the chillun") in a small town ninety miles
from Elktown. Of course, of course . . . .

"Hurry up, Chrystal," called Aunt Eugenia, "you'll
be late for Sunday School if you don't get dressed
right away. Besides, your shoes need polishing.
Hurry now!"

Chrys polished her shoes and then she went upstairs and brushed her hair and changed her dress.
She heard the church bells ringing far away as if in
another town. Even the big bell almost across the
street from her house was no more than a mosquito
buzzing at the edge of her consciousness.

Her mind was busy going over the poems she had
written and wondering if any of them would do. Or
had she better write a new one? She did not have
time to get out the shoe box from under her bed on
the sleeping porch. But she knew most of her poems
by heart. Now she kept saying them over to herself
and trying to fit them into the white space inside the
frame. She almost went off to church without a
hair ribbon.

Cordy had saved a place for her in the Dorcas
Club pew, and Chrys slipped into it absent-

mindedly. Louly was in a class for older girls and
Poo-Bah was still downstairs with the primary
children.

Cordy nudged Chrys and whispered: "I read
something funny on the Children's Page of the
paper this morning." *Cordy, too?* "It said, 'What is
the difference between a cat and a match?' Did you
read the answer?"

"No."

"Well, tell me, then. What is the difference between a cat and a match?"

"I don't know," murmured Chrys dreamily.

"Oh, yes you do. Think! Don't be so dumb," hissed
Cordy.

"Girls! Girls!" said Mrs. Allison. "Open your
Bibles, please."

"Well, I'll tell you the answer, Chrys. A match
lights on its head and a cat lights on its feet. A
match, on its head; a cat, on its feet! Lights! Do you
get it? Isn't that good?"

"Girls, please! Attention now."

"Yes," said Chrys softly, "yes, it's very good." But
all she could see was a blank square of newspaper
surrounded by a narrow black frame, and Cordy
hadn't even noticed it. *Next Sunday in this space
we will print an original poem by one of our young
readers.* The blank square floated before her eyes

like a mirage. It came between her and the pulpit, between her and the tiny print on the page of the Bible, between her and the summer sunlight and green leaves framed in the church door. Chrys felt like a feather, floating around without weight in the summer air. She knew what she had to do. And she had to do it today.

Mrs. Lark had issued a special invitation to the Tucker children to take dinner at her house every Sunday after church as long as their parents were away. So Chrys saw Louly, Ko-Ko, and Poo-Bah go chattering away with Cordy and her brothers. She did not expect to be included because she had a good home of her own and there would probably be stewed chicken with dumplings and fresh peas from the garden, and possibly even a strawberry short-cake. Today she was in such a dream of literary ambition that she scarcely knew or cared what other people were doing around her.

After dinner on a warm Sunday afternoon, Grandma and Aunt Eugenia took naps. The house became so quiet that you could hear the crickets fiddling away in the hot grass beyond the screen door. Every bird chirp sounded like a small explosion in the deep green silence. The whole town seemed to be sleeping. Only Chrys was wide awake, planning and scheming.

She sat on her cot on the sleeping porch and read through all of her poems. Yes, she knew them by heart, but they seemed different when she read them from the scraps of paper on which they were written. They would seem even more different in newspaper print, she knew, and she decided that they were all unworthy.

Chewing the end of her pencil and looking at the ceiling, she began to compose a new poem. She remembered the thought she had had about the mountain stream and the Milky Way. There had never been a moment's time to put it on paper and make it rhyme until now. So now she wrestled with it, shoving it and pulling it and beating it into shape.

> *A mountain stream is falling*
> *Where the wind is calling.*

That was good, Chrys thought, but then she was stuck and she couldn't go on for a long time. Finally she began to write again, very fast:

> *White horses leap and play*
> *In the wild stream's spray.*
> *Their manes and tails are white*
> *Gleaming in starlight.*
> *Perhaps they'll fly away*
> *To join the Milky Way.*

It was not quite what she wanted to say, but she couldn't think of anything better. On the whole, she felt satisfied.

Tiptoeing quietly so that she would not wake up the sleepers, Chrys got a sheet of notepaper, an envelope, and a two-cent stamp from Aunt Eugenia's desk. She sat at the dining table, where she could write very carefully with pen and ink. The kind of scrawl she made when she sat on the edge of her bed with a paper on her lap would not do for this. Very carefully she copied the poem in ink on the heavy notepaper.

It did not take long, even when she worked very slowly and carefully. The eight lines only half filled the note page. They would certainly not fill up the white space in the center of the Children's Page when they were printed in the small black newspaper type.

For a few moments Chrys sat still and thought. She heard the crickets and the bird chirps outside the screen door. Then she leaned over the notepaper again and swiftly drew two trees with something that looked like a stream and waterfall between them. Behind them she put a mountain. With her head on one side she considered her achievement.

"Maybe I am a better artist than I am a poet," she thought. She signed it *Chrystal Reese, aged 13,*

Warsaw, Idaho. Then, feeling very happy and well satisfied, she folded up the paper and put it in the envelope. She addressed the envelope to Aunt Augusta, the Children's Page, in care of the *Elktown Bugle.* She stuck the two-cent stamp in the corner of the envelope, and before she could change her mind, she trotted down to the post office and slipped her letter in the slot.

When she returned, Grandma and Aunt were up from their naps. They were reading the paper in the cool, high-ceilinged parlor.

"Where were you?" Aunt said. "I thought maybe you had gone to Cordy's."

"No," said Chrys, "I went for a walk." For some strange reason she could not bear to tell anyone that she had been so crazy as to send a poem to the newspaper in Elktown.

The enormity of what she had done had struck her as soon as the letter disappeared into the slot in the post-office wall. Perhaps it was the utter impossibility of getting it back that appalled her. Would anyone she knew have done a thing like that? Cordy might have thought about it, but she would never have gone ahead and done it without telling everybody first and getting a lot of good advice. Even Louly, with all of her imagination, would have been too busy and practical to bother with a

poem for the newspaper. Louly might even be scorn-
ful of a person who did, and Chrys could hear
Poo-Bah saying: "Shakespeare's a poet, and doesn't
know it."

Poo-Bah would laugh. There was no one, no one
that Chrys knew, who would expose her inner self
to the whole world by sending a poem to the newspaper. No one, that is, except *Chrystal Reese, aged
13, Warsaw, Idaho.* Aged 13! On the *Children's*
Page!

Chrys went out in the backyard to meditate on
her folly. She went into the barn and stroked
Tommy's soft nose. He whinnied and rubbed
against her, and she turned him out into the horse
lot for a run and gave him a green apple. Then she
climbed up into one of the cherry trees and noticed
that the cherries were almost ripe. Another day or
two and the pie cherries would be ready to pick. The
Royal Anne and the Black Republican cherries would
come about a week later. Then everybody would be
busy picking and canning and making pies, and
Chrys could climb up to a favorite notch in the
branches of the Royal Anne tree where she could
sit reading a book and eating her fill of cherries.
And, of course, they'd never print her poem anyway,
so what was all the fuss about?

Nevertheless, Chrys worried all week. She was

different enough already. She had no regular family, no brothers and sisters, like the other children of town; she was bookish and alone-ish, while they were not; good grades came easy for her, and they made her ashamed. Above all other things Chrys longed to be like everybody else. The family situation could not be changed. She had to live with it. But she need not make herself stranger than ever by doing things nobody else would think of doing. And now, in a fit of madness, she had sent a poem to the newspaper, the *Children*'s Page, and if it was printed, everybody that she knew in the world would see it. "Well, that's just like Chrystal Reese," they would say, "she's so different! A nice little girl, but so different."

In anguish Chrys awaited the following Sunday.

It was some comfort to throw herself into the part of Snoot Rattletrap who would never, under the most extenuating circumstances, have sent a poem to the Sunday paper. They played wildly all week, and toward the end of the week they began to pick the pie cherries. Everybody had a wonderful time except Chrys, who was unusually silent and absent-minded.

Next Sunday morning Chrys was waiting on the front porch when the *Elktown Bugle* was delivered. She did not waste a glance on the funny papers, but opened directly to the Children's Page. Her heart beat wildly as she looked at it. There was the central frame with printing in it. What did it say? Leaning close with her loose hair falling like a screen on either side of her face, Chrys saw that the frame contained three poems instead of one. A wave of relief began to sweep over her.

> *I have a dog whose name is Rover*
> *When he was lost I looked all over*
> *When he came back he waged his tail*
> *My love for him will never fail.*
>
> *Theresa Billings—aged 10*

> *A little old woman lived on a hill*
> *When she got ill*
> *She took a pill.*
>
> *Guy Schumacher—aged 7*

> *Hickery—dicery—dock*
> *I can tell time on a clock*
> *One two*
> *Now I'm threw.*
>
> *Enid Lindstrom—aged 5*

Chrys looked out at the dewy lawn, and the sun lay there so peacefully and bright. The crickets were already beginning to tune their fiddles. What

a marvelous day! Chrys folded the paper as if it had
never been opened and took it indoors.

Aunt Eugenia was making pancakes and Chrys
ate the biggest breakfast she had eaten in a week.

Feeling very much relieved (and only very
slightly disappointed deep down inside), Chrys said
to herself: "What perfectly terrible poems! What if
mine had been there with them!" But Chrys was
honest and she added, "Of course, mine wasn't
really much better, and I am older. The first one I
thought up on the night when Louly made us hear a
mountain stream—that one was a better poem,
even if it didn't rhyme."

She sang as she polished her shoes and brushed
her hair for church. A heavy weight was lifted from
her spirits.

9 · Cherry Pies and Serenades

"Did you see that dumb new thing they have on the Children's Page?" whispered Cordy when Chrys slid into the pew beside her. "Stupid poems by little kids instead of a puzzle picture!"

"Yes, I saw," said Chrys.

"I suppose we're getting too old for the Children's Page anyway," said Cordy. "But I do like the puzzles and the riddles still."

"Now, girls, *please*," said Mrs. Allison.

The cherries ripened fast that week—millions of them, it seemed. Camp was abandoned and Miss Silverbottom and the Rattletraps were forgotten while the girls picked cherries. The Larks had even more fruit trees in their yard than Chrys's grandma had, and Ko-Ko and all of the Lark boys were busy picking too. The going rate for pickers was five cents a bucket and a reasonable amount of eating as they picked. How many buckets could one pick in an hour? The rivalry was intense. But sometimes it was just so much fun to climb to the top of a tree and look off over the rooftops that the reward of five cents a bucket seemed unimportant.

Mrs. Lark and the hired girl and Aunt Eugenia and Grandma were busy washing and cooking the fruit and putting it up in Mason jars for next winter's desserts.

Aunt Eugenia said to Louly, "Would you like to learn how to can cherries, so that you can have some jars of fruit for next winter as a surprise for your mother?"

"Oh, yes," said Louly, "I'd like that. Wouldn't she be surprised? And I'd like to learn how to make cherry pies too."

"We'll help," offered Cordy and Chrys.

Poo-Bah preferred to continue climbing trees with

the boys. But the three older girls transferred their activities to the hot moist kitchens with their pleasant odors of warm sugar and boiling fruit.

Louly learned how to make pie crust, while Cordy and Chrys took turns working the cherry pitter that poked the seeds out of the cherries before they were put into pies.

"Put in lots of sugar, Louly," Cordy advised.

"And lots of dabs of butter on top of the cherries and sugar," added Chrys.

Louly made two pies, and when they had baked slowly for nearly an hour, the girls crowded around to see them come out of the oven. Even Poo-Bah was there by that time, drawn no doubt by the delicious smell. The pies were perfectly golden and flaky with little bubbles of crimson juice oozing out of the slits Louly had cut in the crust. Aunt Eugenia made her air slits like a feather, but Louly made hers like a pine tree.

"The pies are beautiful," the girls said. "How soon can we eat them?"

"Not until they are cold," Louly said. "And then only one today. I'll save the other one for tomorrow."

So that night the most important part of their dinner was the dessert, and it was as good as it looked.

That night another strange and exciting thing

happened. The girls had been asleep in the tent for an hour or two when suddenly Billy began to bark. Chrys came wide awake in an instant and lay tense and silent, listening. She could hear suppressed laughter, then someone speaking softly to Billy. Billy stopped barking and Chrys could imagine him wagging his tail as if he had met a friend. Still it was rather frightening to know that someone was outside the tent in the moonlight. Who could it be? Tentatively Chrys put out a hand and touched Cordy.

"Do you hear what I hear?"

"Yes, someone is outside."

"S-sh!" said Louly. Poo-Bah slept on.

Then all of a sudden came the sound of a guitar and boys' voices began to sing:

> *"Soft o'er the fountain*
> *Ling'ring falls the southern moon,*
> *Far o'er the mountain*
> *Breaks the day too soon!"*

"It couldn't be Ko-Ko," whispered Chrys.

"Or any of my brothers," said Cordy.

"S-s-sh!" said Louly.

> *" 'Nita—wa-a-anita,*
> *Ask your soul if we should part!*

'*Nita—wa-a-anita,*
Lean thou on my heart!"

"Eddie Wendell," hissed Chrys.

"Indubitably!"

"S-s-sh!"

After "Juanita," the serenaders sang "Shine On, Harvest Moon," "Drink to Me Only with Thine Eyes" and "Beautiful Dreamer."

"Should we clap?" asked Cordy.

"No! No! No!" whispered Louly. "S-s-sh!"

> "*Good night, ladies,*
> *Good night, ladies,*
> *Good night, ladies,*
> *We're going to leave you now.*
> *Merrily we roll along,*
> *Roll along, roll along.*
> *Merrily we roll along*
> *Over the deep blue sea.*"

"Aren't you even going to clap *now*?"

"No," whispered Louly.

When the singing was over, a voice near the tent wall said, "Louly! Do you hear? I've got to see you for a minute tomorrow morning, Louly."

Louly did not say a word, but after the singers had departed, she breathed a long sigh.

"Oh, wasn't it lovely?" she murmured. "Were you ever serenaded before, any of you?"

"Of course not," said Chrys and Cordy together. "What do you think?"

"I never was either," Louly said, "but now I have been, just like a Spanish señorita. Oh, wasn't it dreamy and creamy?"

"If you like to hear cats howling on the back fence, it was," said Cordy.

Just then Poo-Bah woke up.

"What are you talking about in the middle of the night?" she wanted to know.

"Oh, you missed it, Poo-Bah! You missed the serenade!"

"Oh, gee-whillicans!" mourned Poo-Bah.

"Go to sleep, all of you chillun," Louly said softly. " 'Twas all a dream. But wasn't it lovely while it lasted?"

The next morning Eddie came around right after breakfast. Louly had put on a neat white middy blouse instead of her old calico apron and her hair was smoothly brushed. Everybody's face was washed. No one mentioned the serenade.

"Why, Eddie, what evah brings you into town today?" asked Louly as if she were greatly surprised to see him.

"My uncle let me take a day off," Eddie said, "because yesterday was my mother's birthday. But I wanted to see you about something else, Louly, before I went back."

"Shall *we* scram out of here?" asked Cordy, and Chrys said, "We can take a walk."

"I'm not going," Poo-Bah said. "I didn't hear the serenade and I'm not going to miss this."

"No, no," Eddie said, "you kids can stay. I just wanted to tell Louly about the speech contest."

"Speech contest?" repeated Louly eagerly. Chrys could almost see Louly's romantic dreams vanishing in even more exciting visions of speaking a piece to a clamoring audience.

"Yes," Eddie said. "I thought you'd want to know that there is going to be a speech contest for the whole county over at Springdale where I work. They are going to give a silver loving cup for the best recitation."

"A silver loving cup!" breathed Louly. "But who can enter?"

"Contestants from all of the summer-session high schools are coming. Louly, I thought you would win it if anybody could."

"But we aren't having a summer session at Warsaw High School this year," Louly said, "and Daddy is away, and I don't s'pose they'd even let me enter at all."

"There's a dance afterward," said Eddie wistfully. "I thought, if you could wangle it somehow, I'd take you to the dance, Louly."

"Oh, Eddie, I'd simply adore it," Louly said. "And a silver loving cup!"

"Of course, she can't go," said Poo-Bah. "Mother and Daddy aren't here, and high school is closed. And besides, the rest of us couldn't go to the dance, and where would we stay overnight?"

"Well, my aunt said that Louly could stay overnight with her," said Eddie.

"But what about us?" asked Poo-Bah, pointing to Cordy and Chrys.

"Poo-Bah," said Louly, "will you please be quiet for a minute and let me do some of the talking?"

"I was just trying to be helpful," Poo-Bah said.

"Eddie, it's very kind of your aunt, and I would love to go, but how would I get there?"

"It's only twenty miles, Louly, and the train goes every day, or you can drive it with a horse and buggy. I'd come and pick you up, but it's on a Saturday and that's the busiest day at the store."

"I have a horse and buggy," Cordy said, "and maybe Mama could chaperone us."

"Maybe I could take Tommy," ventured Chrys, "but he's pretty slow. We'd have to start awfully early."

"But I don't know why we are talking about this at all," said Louly. "I'm not going to high school this summer, and so far as I know Warsaw High School hasn't been invited to participate, and Daddy is away and everything."

"Well, look," said Eddie, "I brought you the name and address of the speech teacher at Springdale who is in charge of the contest. Why don't you write to him and find out? The contest is several weeks away. There's a lot of time. I just happened to hear about it, and I remembered 'Barbara Frietchie,' and I thought you could do it again just the way you did it on the Fourth of July and you'd be sure to win."

"Oh, no!" Louly cried. "It would have to be something different, something very special. I'd work up a new one completely."

"Well, go ahead and write to the speech teacher, Louly, and lots of good luck! I've got to run now, because I have to get back to work as soon as I can."

"Oh, Eddie, wait a minute," Louly said. "Do you like cherry pie?"

"I sure do," said Eddie.

"Wait, then!" cried Louly. She ran into the house

and came back with the remaining cherry pie wrapped in a clean white towel. "Take this, Eddie. I made it myself."

Poo-Bah began to open her mouth for a noisy protest, but Chrys saw her just in time and clapped her hand over Poo-Bah's mouth.

"Thank you, Louly. I didn't know you could cook too!" said Eddie.

"She's quite accomplished," said Cordy generously. "She makes up all of our plays."

"And, Eddie," said Louly, "the serenade was lovely. I'll never forget it."

"Oh, it wasn't much. Some of us fellows were out singing and we just thought—well, good-by, Louly. See you at the speech contest."

"Good-by, Eddie. I'll do my best."

When he was gone, Chrys removed her hand from Poo-Bah's mouth, and Poo-Bah grumbled, "Well, I thought that cherry pie was intended for *us*."

"Poo-Bah," cried Cordy, "you aren't very romantical, are you?"

"Give her time," said Chrys. "She may grow up like us or maybe even like Louly, if we give her time."

Louly was too busy with her thoughts to pay any attention to them. "A silver loving cup!" she said.

She read the address that Eddie had left in her hands: *Mr. Peter Spiegel, Instructor in Speech, James Russell Lowell High School, Springdale, Idaho.*

"I'll have to write him a letter," Louly said, "but what shall I say? Shall I tell him that my father's in the East and we aren't having any summer school at Warsaw High, but that I would like to come to speak a piece in his contest just the same?"

"Of course not!" Cordy said.

"No, of course not!" repeated Louly. "This will have to be handled with tact!"

"We'll help you all we can," offered Poo-Bah.

"No, please," said Louly. "All of you go and pit cherries or climb trees or something, and let me think. I'll read you the letter before I send it."

Reluctantly the three younger girls left Louly sitting at her father's desk in his upstairs study. She had a lot of scratch paper laid out to practice on, and waiting at one side were a couple of clean white sheets of official letter paper on which were printed:

Warsaw Public School System
Warsaw, Idaho
Warsaw High School   Office of the Principal
Gideon C. Tucker, Ph.D.

"Are you going to use *that?*" asked Chrys in awe.

"What else?" asked Louly.

By three o'clock in the afternoon, the children could restrain their curiosity no longer. Louly had not appeared for lunch, and they had eaten bologna sandwiches and milk on Chrys's side porch.

"She's had plenty of time," said Poo-Bah.

"If she hasn't done it yet, she never will," said Chrys.

"Let's serenade her," said Cordy.

As they approached the Tucker house, they could hear a clatter of pans in the kitchen.

"I think she's making another cherry pie," said Poo-Bah.

The three girls lined up beside the kitchen door and began to sing:

> *"Can she make a cherry pie,*
> *Billy Boy? Billy Boy?*
> *Can she make a cherry pie,*
> *Charming Billy?*
> *She can make a cherry pie*
> *Quick as you can wink an eye,*
> *She's a young thing,*
> *She cannot leave her mother."*

"All right," said Louly, coming to the door with floury hands, "I'm making you another pie, and I've written the letter, and I hope that everything is all settled."

They crowded around to read the letter. It was very beautifully written in ink on the official stationery. It said:

Mr. Peter Spiegel
Instructor in Speech
James Russell Lowell High School
Springdale, Ida.

Dear Sir:

At the behest of our principal, Gideon C. Tucker, Ph.D., I am writing to inquire about the speech contest to be held in your city. I understand that a silver loving cup will be presented to the person giving the best recitation. If high schools throughout the county are to be represented, we feel very strongly that Warsaw High School should be among their number. In fact, we have a candidate whose credentials are of the highest caliber, and we should be proud to see her entered in your competition.

Please advise us as to time and conditions.

Respectfully yours,
(Miss) Permeliar Silverbottom,
Secretary to Mr. Tucker

Telephone—Warsaw 705

"Well, what do you think?" asked Louly.

"It's superb," said Chrys. "Do you really think he'll telephone?"

"I hope so."

"But *Permeliar Silverbottom!*" objected Cordy. "Isn't that a little wild?"

"I think it will impress him," Louly said.

"You've said it beautifully, Louly," said Chrys, "all that about the candidate with credentials of the highest caliber."

"I know," Louly said, "the wastebasket is full of wrong starts and I had to keep going to the dictionary to find out how to spell things. And don't tell me that *caliber* should be spelled *calibre*, because the dick says that either one is all right, so I took the first one."

"Well, it's a masterpiece," said Chrys, "that part about at the behest of! It doesn't say that your father isn't here, and it sounds just right."

"That's what I thought," said Louly complacently.

"But I don't know what Daddy would say," objected Poo-Bah. "Maybe he wouldn't like it."

"Well, he wouldn't want Warsaw High to be unrepresented in a county contest, now would he?" demanded Louly. "You have to think of that. We're sort of like his representatives while he is gone."

"All right," Poo-Bah said. "How soon do you s'pose we'll get an answer? And what shall we wear to Springdale on the night of the contest? I think middy blouses will not be fancy enough. I suppose our Sunday dresses."

"Don't go too fast," Louly said. "Mr. Spiegel hasn't answered yet—in fact, the letter hasn't even been mailed."

Chrys had a momentary shudder of dread at the thought of a letter vanishing down a slot at the post office and being lost beyond recall.

"Maybe you'd better think about it for a while, Louly," she said.

But Louly was flushed with triumph and confident happiness.

"I *have* thought about it," she said, "and it gives me goose pimples all up and down my spine."

10 · Zingarella

In the excitement of cherry season and the serenade and the letter to Springdale, Chrys had almost forgotten her anxiety about the Children's Page of the *Elktown Bugle*. There had only been that one bad moment when she visualized Louly's letter disappearing in the greedy mouth of the post office slot as her own letter had done. This shook her briefly and then she thought, "But the paper didn't print my poem. They want the poems of *little* kids. I really don't have to worry at all."

The other girls helped Louly store the jars of canned fruit she had made on the shelves in the Tuckers' cellar.

"Mama will be pleased and proud," said Louly. "She didn't expect anything like this."

"And if you win the silver loving cup for Warsaw High, I guess Daddy will be proud of you too," said Poo-Bah. "He wouldn't expect that either."

"Well, kidlets," said Louly gaily, "we won't count our chickens until they are hatched. But just the same, I've got to begin learning a new recitation— something bang-up, splendid and dramatic. I'm going down to the library this afternoon. Anybody want to go along?"

The Carnegie Library was a small gray stone building with steps and pillars. It looked very much like hundreds of other small Carnegie libraries in hundreds of other small towns all over the United States. Chrys knew all about Andrew Carnegie because he was a Scotsman as her father had been. But Mr. Carnegie was also very rich, and had a Scotsman's belief in the power of books and learning to elevate a new nation; so he had given all of these libraries to towns that might never have been able to afford a public library without his help.

Chrys loved the smell of the Carnegie Library— a smell of floor wax and paste and old books, and something else that could only be anticipation and mystery and wonder at what was hidden between the covers of the many unread books. She went to the library often by herself (another way in which she was different from the other girls of the town), and one of her fondest, unspoken ambitions was to be chosen some summer as the librarian's assistant. Miss Crandall, the librarian, had a younger sister who acted as her assistant every summer. Chrys felt that Ellie Crandall couldn't possibly care as much about being a librarian's assistant as she herself would have done, but she had never plucked up the courage to ask Miss Crandall if she needed more help. One of Chrys's problems was that when she most wanted something for herself, she found it hardest to confide in anyone. With Louly it was quite different. If Louly wanted something, she said so right away. It was not that she was selfish or egotistical, but just that she did not mind letting other people know how she was feeling inside. Louly had no closed doors, but Chrystal Reese had a good many little doors inside herself that could not be opened by other people's latchkeys.

"Miss Crandall," said Louly, "where are the books of recitations and poems?"

"I know," said Chrys.

"Yes, I expect you do," said Miss Crandall, "I've seen you sitting there very often. They're over by the window on the shelf marked POETRY."

"You see, Miss Crandall," said Louly, "I may be having to give a recitation, and I want something very dramatic and exciting. I thought maybe you could suggest something."

"I heard that you gave a very good recitation on the Fourth of July," Miss Crandall said, "but I suppose you want something different this time."

"Yes, different, but even more dramatic and exciting."

Miss Crandall left her desk and went over to the poetry shelf. She drew out a fat volume called *The Complete Elocutionist*. "This is good," she said, "because it has illustrations and diagrams and shows you just how to use your eyebrows and make proper gestures with your arms and hands."

"Oh, I can do that part myself," said Louly confidently. "All I need is an exciting poem."

The girls all took books and sat around the "little folks" table, looking for poems. The library was very quiet. On this bright summer day most people preferred to be outdoors.

"Here's 'The Village Blacksmith,' " said Cordy.

"No, no," said Louly, "everybody knows that one. I want something fancier."

"Here's 'How They Brought the Good News from Ghent to Aix,' " said Chrys. "I love the way that one starts:

"I sprang to the stirrup, and Joris, and he;
I galloped, Dirck galloped, we galloped all three.

Can't you hear them galloping, Louly? You could make the whole audience get up on their chairs and start galloping."

"You girls are too fond of horses," Louly said. "I don't want to make the audience gallop away and leave me standing there all by myself. Be quiet a minute now. I think I've found one." She was reading through the last selection in *The Complete Elocutionist*. A footnote under the poem said: *"This is a very difficult selection and should be undertaken only by the most advanced students."* To say a thing like that to Louly was to issue a challenge which she could not resist. The poem was called "Zingarella or the Gypsy Bride."

Louly read through it silently, but they could tell by the way she tossed her head or frowned or made little gestures with her hands that she was already trying it out in her mind and finding it exciting.

"Yes, that's it!" she said when she had finished reading. She popped out of her chair and took the book up to the librarian's desk. "I'd like to check this book out, please, Miss Crandall."

"It didn't take you long," Miss Crandall said.

"No, it didn't," Louly said. "I like to do things fast. It's the hardest one in the book."

"Well, good luck to you, dearie."

The other girls crammed their books back on the shelves and ran after Louly.

"It's got everything," Louly said as they walked homeward. "It starts with thunder and lightning. I know the first two lines already:

"Loud rolled the thunder, lightning rent the sky;
The gypsy camp in midnight darkness lay—

And it's got this mysterious old gypsy woman reading the cards by the flickering light of the campfire, and the young nobleman in love with the beautiful gypsy girl, and his haughty father, and the young gypsy man who is also in love with Zingarella, and there is a fight with swords, 'flashing in the firelight,' and then the old woman reads the cards and she sees—she sees that Zingarella is really the sister of the young nobleman who was stolen in infancy. I mean Zingarella was stolen, not the young nobleman, if you follow me."

"We follow you," panted the younger girls running along at Louly's heels. They did not wish to lose a word.

"And now that Zingarella has a wonderful future in a nobleman's castle opening out before her, what does she do?"

"She asks for an ice-cream soda," suggested Poo-Bah.

"She removes her gypsy rags and takes a bath and puts on a beautiful gown of blue satin sewn with pearls," said Cordy.

"She decides to marry her gypsy sweetheart and stay with the gypsies," said Chrys dreamily.

"Why, Chrys, how did you guess?" cried Louly.

"I just knew it in my inmost soul," said Chrys.

"Seems to me," remarked Cordy, "this sounds something like the novel Chrys and I wrote last winter. You know, *The Romantical Perils of Lester and Lynette.*"

"Well, it's not like that at all, I can tell you," Louly said. "Wait until you hear me recite it. Your hair will stand right up on your head. It's that kind of poem, and I'll give it everything I've got."

Chrys overslept on Sunday morning. Aunt Eugenia had to come and shake her to wake her up in time to eat oatmeal before Sunday School. As she went sleepily to the table she saw that someone had already brought in the *Elktown Bugle* and put it beside Grandma's chair. She would have unfolded it and taken a quick look at the Children's Page just to make sure, but Aunt said: "Hurry now, darling. It's almost time for the first church bells to ring. I let you sleep as long as I could. You girls don't get enough rest on the hard, cold ground in that miserable tent. I should think you'd be tired of that camping game by now."

Chrys devoted herself to the hot oatmeal with sugar and cream. It tasted delicious.

"I *am* a little tired of bacon and raw fries," Chrys said, "but we aren't ready to stop camping yet."

"And how about your shoes?" Aunt said. "I'm sure they need polishing."

"I left them over at Tuckers', I think. We all went barefoot after we came back from the library."

"Well, hurry and get them. For three big girls, you act very much like little folks. It's all right for Poo-Bah to kick off her shoes and go barefoot. She's only ten, but you—you're almost as old as Louly."

"Louly did it too."

"I know. Sometimes I wonder if she *is* so responsible—"

Aunt Eugenia rarely scolded and lectured except on Sunday morning. It was as if she were getting in the right mood for listening to a sermon on Pre-destination and Damnation. Grandma didn't say anything, but Chrys could see that she was sitting in her patent rocker reading the *Elktown Bugle*.

The first Sunday School bells began to ring as Chrys ran out of the side door to go to the Tuckers'. Before she had crossed the driveway, the back screen door of the Tuckers' house banged open, and Louly and Poo-Bah in their Sunday finery burst out. Even Ko-Ko, in a clean collar and a necktie, was right behind them.

"Chrys, it's beautiful!" cried Louly.

"Shakespeare's a poet," began Poo-Bah.

Chrys stopped in her tracks like a stag at bay. They were carrying a sheet of newspaper—the Children's Page of the *Elktown Bugle!*

"Oh, no!" Chrys cried in despair.

"You're all over the page," said Ko-Ko with a friendly grin.

"No, no!" said Chrys.

"Why didn't you tell us you had sent a poem to the paper?" cried Louly.

"And he doesn't know it," finished Poo-Bah breathlessly.

Louly held out the paper for Chrys to see. There it was, her poem, the only one in the black frame in the middle of the page, and some unknown magician had blown up her drawing of trees, river, and mountain to twice its size.

By Chrystal Reese, aged 13, Warsaw, Idaho. Chrys felt as if she would sink into the ground. A strange pink haze swam before her eyes.

"Give it here!" she cried. "Give it here!" She snatched the paper out of Louly's hand and tore it in two. Then, as she was turning to run back home, Aunt Eugenia came rushing down the porch steps.

"My darling, darling little girl," she said, "you have a poem in the paper. Why didn't you tell us? What a lovely surprise! Aunty is so proud! Isn't it lovely?"

"No, no!" cried Chrys, not knowing where to turn next. It seemed as if they had cut off all avenues of escape. She seized the sheet of paper that Aunt Eugenia held in her hand and tore that in two also. Then she ran blindly up the porch steps past Grandma, who had come out to join the celebration. With the ragged sheets of paper still crumpled in her hands she ran for the seclusion of her sleeping porch. But before she was out of earshot she heard Louly saying, "Whatever is the matter with her?"

And Grandma said: "Leave her alone for a while. She'll feel better later."

Chrys shut and locked the door to the sleeping porch. She lay down on her unmade cot and pulled the pillow over her head to shut out the daylight. She thought that she had never felt more miserable in all her life before.

After a while Louly came around the house and stood near the screen under the honey locust tree.

"Why, Chrys," she said, "we're all real proud of you. Think of having a poem and a drawing in the newspaper!"

"I don't care!" said Chrys in a pillow-muffled voice. She did care, but she couldn't think of anything else to say just then.

"You aren't mad, are you? Did we do something wrong?"

"No! No! No!" said Chrys. "Please go away, Louly."

Louly went away. The second bell for Sunday School rang and from the church across the street came the faint sound of organ and hymns.

When Chrys was sure that everyone else was in church, she got up and put on her riding skirt and her old sweater. She went to the barn and saddled Tommy. Rowdy yelped with delight and Tommy arched his neck and capered. "If I could live with animals and never see another human being, I would be perfectly happy," said Chrys to herself.

She rode out the back driveway, away from the church, and headed for the open fields beyond town.

11 · Chrys's Bad Day

Dust lay on the last wild roses blooming along the rail fences, and the oat fields had turned a pale silver yellow. The wheat fields that rolled away over the many little foothills leading to the mountains would soon be pure gold. The mountains themselves were blue and mysterious.

Chrys knew the name of every flower and weed that grew along the wayside. She loved the clear, bright air, and the way the morning sunlight lay on the irregular folds of the hills. She let the pony take his own way, and if he saw a particularly nice thistle blossom by the roadside, she let him stop and pick it. He liked thistle blossoms almost as much as peanut brittle, and he had a special way of opening his mouth wide and folding it around the thistle so that the spines did not stick him before he chewed them up.

Chrys could always think better on horseback than anywhere else. "Human beings on two legs are only half as good as human beings on horses," she often told herself. She liked to read the old myths about the centaurs who were half man and half horse, and she thought that she would have liked to be a centaur.

At first she would not allow herself to think about the poem that had been delivered on everybody's front porch that morning. She thought instead about how the wild roses were nearly gone and the goldenrod and asters would soon be beginning, how the little creek had dried up and how tufts of blue lobelia were blooming in the cracked mud of the stream bed where water had rushed down in the springtime.

Then into her mind popped her picture of pine trees and stream and mountain. She had not taken time to look at it carefully, but even the one hasty glance had told her that when they had made it so large they had somehow exaggerated all of the odd and crooked lines, so that it did not look as well as it had when it was small.

"I'll have to study and learn how to draw better," Chrys thought.

She remembered the rage of ambitious hurry that she had been in just two weeks ago when she had written her poem out in ink and drawn her picture and mailed the letter. "I must have been crazy," she thought.

And why was she so ashamed now? She didn't really know. It was a mystery that she could not explain away, but it was true. The feeling was so bad that it actually hurt her somewhere in her chest. "Perhaps I shall die of it," Chrys thought, but then, of course, she knew that she would not. Instead she would have to go on living and pretending that nothing unusual had happened. She would have to face all of her friends, and if they said anything about her poem in the newspaper, she would say, "Poem? What poem? Please don't mention it again. I don't remember any poem."

Chrys came back from her ride feeling refreshed and renewed. Her chest still hurt when she thought of her poem, but she had a good appetite for stewed chicken and cherry pie.

Grandma and Aunt Eugenia said nothing to her about the newspaper, but Aunt Eugenia looked at her oddly and almost as if she were on the edge of tears.

Chrys hardened her heart.

The Tuckers were all over at the Larks' for the rest of the day and doubtless they were looking at the Larks' *Elktown Bugle* and saying, "Chrys is certainly funny, the way she acted this morning. But then she's different. Who else would have a poem on the Children's Page and never tell anyone she had done it either?"

Chrys spent a quiet afternoon. She cut some of the small yellow roses that grew on the trellis near the front door and arranged them nicely in the gold-fish bowl and put them on top of the bookcase. She got out the mythology book and read about centaurs. After a while she went into the sleeping porch, where her bed was still unmade.

On the floor under the bed were the pieces of torn and crumpled newspaper. She picked them up, without really looking at them, and folded them carefully. Then she put them into the shoe box with the old spelling tablet, the pencil, and all the other treasures that had once meant so much to her.

"I'll never look at them again," Chrys said to herself.

She made her bed up neatly, and because there was nothing better to do, she lay down to take a nap. Before she went to sleep, she remembered a yellowed clipping that Grandma had pasted in her cookbook:

TWENTY-ONE WAYS TO USE OLD NEWSPAPERS
1. to wrap the garbage
2. to line the canary's cage
3. sewed in the lining of the winter coat to keep out cold
4. folded on the windowsill to keep out sifting snow
5. in the bottom of the cat's dirt box
6. if tightly rolled they may be burned in the fireplace instead of logs.

Chrys could not remember any more of the twenty-one ways, but these were enough. Now she lay there imagining her poem wrapped around the garbage, sewed into somebody's coat, in the bottom of the canary's cage, or lining the cat's dirt box. It was like counting sheep. In a minute she was asleep.

About four o'clock Aunt Eugenia came to wake Chrys up and say that Mrs. Corwin and Ethel had come to call, and would she please come out as soon as she could to entertain Ethel?

Mrs. Corwin was a dreary old lady, full of complaints about her health, and Ethel was her stepdaughter and a person Chrys detested. Mrs. Corwin was very fat and wheezy, and Ethel was very thin and sniffy. The only thing they had in common was a critical attitude which made them find fault with almost everything except themselves. When she saw them coming Chrys usually ran out the back door and escaped. But today she was trapped. She took a long time brushing her hair, and then she went reluctantly into the parlor.

As she came in, Chrys heard Aunt Eugenia saying, "Did you see the *Elktown Bugle* today, Mrs. Corwin?"

Chrys stood frozen in the doorway listening.

"No," Mrs. Corwin said. "We don't take the Sunday paper. It's sacrilegious, I think—all those dreadful comic pictures when folks' minds should be on higher things. No, we never take the *Elktown Bugle*, do we, Ethel?"

"No, Mama. We never look at it!"

For an instant Chrystal loved them. She came into the parlor, and said, "Well, hello, Ethel. How do you do, Mrs. Corwin?"

"Not very well, dear, thank you," Mrs. Corwin said. "I have been having sciatica very badly in my left hip. You wouldn't think it would trouble me in summer weather, but my flesh is frail. I'm not like other people."

Inwardly Chrys groaned. Mrs. Corwin too?

"Would you like to come out in the backyard, Ethel?" Chrys asked. "I think there may be some cherries left."

"Thank you, Chrystal," Ethel said, "but cherries give me the hives."

Ethel was about the age of Louly, but, oh, what a difference there was! Chrys tried again. "Would you like to see the pony or swing in the hammock or something?"

"Not unless you want to, Chrystal. Mama and I came by to visit with your aunty and grandma. Your aunty has promised to show me a new tatting pattern."

"On *Sunday?*" asked Chrys in mock astonishment.

"Oh, I don't mind tatting on Sunday," Ethel said. "It's sewing bloomers and aprons and dish towels that's wrong on Sunday, I believe."

"Yes, dear," Aunt Eugenia said. "Let me get my tatting shuttle and I'll show you. Chrys never would learn to tat, and it's nice to teach someone who really wants to learn."

"I'm very eager," Ethel said. "I'm quite surprised that Chrystal should not care to learn to tat."

"Well, she does many other lovely things," said Aunt Eugenia loyally.

"I didn't see her at church or Sunday School today," said Ethel.

"No, I went horseback riding," said Chrys in an unnecessarily loud voice.

"Tsk! Tsk! Tsk!" said both Ethel and Mrs. Corwin.

"Here, Ethel dear," said Aunt Eugenia, "you hold the shuttle like this, and wrap the thread around your fingers, so—"

Chrys sat in silent boredom while Ethel learned the new tatting pattern, and while Grandma and Mrs. Corwin discussed weather and fruit canning and the various diseases that had afflicted Mrs. Corwin during a long and varied lifetime. At least the *Elktown Bugle* was not mentioned again, and Chrys was thankful for that.

"What a lot of funny people there are in the world!" Chrys thought to herself. "And, of course, I'm one of them." That thought should have made her happier, but it didn't. She wanted more than ever to be just like the regular people, the ones who were not "funny."

Mrs. Corwin and Ethel stayed for tea and cookies.

"But we don't have caraway seeds on *our* cookies," Ethel said. "Why do you?"

"Well, Grandma likes them that way," said Chrys.

"I don't much care about caraway seeds myself. They look like little black bugs on top of the cookies, don't you think?"

"Oh, *ish!*" said Ethel. "How could you *say* that, Chrystal? Now you've spoiled my whole tea, and I was looking forward to it so much!"

"Here, Ethel dear," said Aunt Eugenia, "here are some cookies that don't have caraway seeds on top. Try one of these."

"Perhaps I'd better not, thanks, not after what Chrystal just said. But I will have another lump of sugar in my tea, please."

When Mrs. Corwin and Ethel had departed, Chrys went out and sat on the cement mounting block in front of the house. She heard Louly and Cordy and Poo-Bah coming back from the Larks' with their arms full of camping things. She could hear them as soon as they passed the courthouse, because they were laughing and chattering so gaily. She thought of running indoors and hiding herself, but they sounded so wonderful, so dear, so unlike Ethel Corwin, that she couldn't help running to meet them.

"Do you know what, Chrys?" said Cordy.

"No, what?"

"Oh, it's the most wonderful news," said Louly.

"Let me tell first," said Poo-Bah.

"What? What is it?" gasped Chrys.

"It's about the speech contest," said Louly. "*If* we get to go, that is."

"Yes?"

"Cordy's mother has promised to take us on the train and to chaperone us, and we can stay overnight in the Springdale Hotel. Think of staying overnight in a hotel! Won't it be exciting?"

"And did she think it was all right, your writing the letter and everything?"

"Yes, she thought it was all right if the Springdale people agreed. And she was sure that Louly's father wouldn't mind."

"So now all we have to do is hear from Springdale."

"And maybe Ko-Ko and Cordy's brothers will go, if they can get a horse or earn money for train fare."

"And me, too?" asked Chrys, still wondering how different she really was. "Am I to go too?"

"Indubitably!" they cried. "For goodness' sakes! We wouldn't go without you, Chrys!"

"Oh, good!" said Chrys with a deep sigh. She was still one of them after all.

12 · Good-by, Miss Silverbottom

There were moments when Chrys wondered if it would not have been better to talk about her poem in the *Elktown Bugle*. But no one ever mentioned it to her again. Sometimes she caught them looking at her oddly, and that was almost worse than hearing them talk about it.

Louly was full of business that week. On Monday morning she started right in.

"We need to houseclean," she said. "And we've let the garden grow up to weeds. Everything is in a mess, and it's high time that we all got busy and cleaned it. We must be responsible. Where is Ko-Ko this morning?"

"He's taken the lawn mower over to Witters' to mow their lawn for them," said Poo-Bah.

"Witters' lawn!" cried Louly indignantly. "And look at *our* lawn! He hasn't mowed it for two weeks."

"Well, Mrs. Witter *pays* him for mowing their lawn."

"Then *he* can pay *us* for mowing *this* lawn for *him*," said Louly. "You run over to Witters' and tell him that, Poo-Bah. Tell him that as soon as he brings the lawn mower back we'll use it here and he can pay us twenty-five cents an hour. And in the meantime Cordy and Chrys and I will start to wash the windows and turn out the closets."

"Oh, Louly," protested Cordy and Chrys, but Louly was firm. She worked harder than anyone else, and all the while she was reciting bits of "Zingarella or the Gypsy Bride."

"Dark as the midnight raven's wing, her hair
Was banded black with strands of scarlet silk!

Cordy, undo the window latch and lift it up."

Cordy opened the window, but her mind was on the gypsy bride.

"Louly, what kind of poetry is that anyway?" asked Cordy. "It doesn't rhyme."

"It says in the book that it's iambic pentameter, and it's called heroic blank verse. It's the way Shakespeare wrote."

Chrys busied herself in Mrs. Tucker's closet, putting the shoes in a neat line and dusting the floor. She had nothing to say about poetry today, and Poo-Bah was not there to chant, "Shakespeare's a poet, and doesn't know it."

But a few minutes later Poo-Bah arrived with the news that Ko-Ko would be back to mow the lawn just as soon as he finished at the Witters'.

"He didn't like the idea of paying us at all," she laughed. "He said, '*Me* pay *you*? With my hard-earned money?' I think he and Cordy's brothers are earning money to go on the train to Springdale when Louly speaks her piece, *if* they let her speak it. Matt and Vince are down the street mowing lawns at Smithers' place."

"Oh, dear!" said Louly with a worried frown. She began to recite softly:

> "*The fortune teller lifted clawlike hands,*
> '*I read ill fortune in the cards,' she said.*"

Then she added, "And you, Poo-Bah, go get a dusting rag."

"Louly," said Cordy, "I've noticed something."

"What have you noticed, Cordy? Let me hear."

"There, you did it again," said Cordy. "You're talking in heroic blank verse, Louly. Listen to this: 'And *you*, Poo-*Bah*, go *get* a *dust*ing *rag*.' 'What *have* you *no*ticed, *Cord*y? *Let* me *hear*.' It's just like 'The *for*tune *tell*er *lift*ed *claw*like *hands*.' Chrys, you are the poet. What do you think? Is Louly talking that kind of pentameter thing?"

Chrys was reaching up to knock down a cobweb in the top of Mrs. Tucker's closet. Her elbow jarred a cardboard box on one of the shelves, and it tumbled down, spilling the contents all over the closet floor. The box had been full of bright-colored scarves and pieces of silk, and now Chrys stood in the middle of an untidy sea of color. Cordy forgot that she was waiting for Chrys to answer. "Well, there are the scarlet strands," she cried, "to tie up her raven-wing hair. Tell it to us in heroic verse, Louly."

"Oh, it's Mama's piece box," Louly said in her ordinary voice. "Mama started saving bright-colored pieces when she was a little girl, to make a crazy quilt—"

"A *which* quilt?"

"A crazy quilt," said Louly. "Crazy quilts were like patchwork quilts except that, instead of having regular squares or triangles, the pieces were all cut up into irregular shapes and sewed together with fancy stitches and they were made of many-colored silks. Mama used to let us dress up in the colored scarves and pieces when we were little because she said she might never get around to making the quilt anyhow."

"So now we can all be gypsies," Poo-Bah said. "I speak for the yellow one with purple spots."

The girls began tying gaudily colored pieces about their heads or draping them over their shoulders. They crowded around Mrs. Tucker's mirror to admire themselves.

"I speak to be Zingarella," Poo-Bah cried.

"No!" said Cordy. "Louly must be Zingarella. It's her recitation. I'll be her gypsy lover, and Chrys can be the young nobleman who turns out to be her long-lost brother. What are their names, Louly?"

"Amadeo is the gypsy and Sir Oliver Trent is the nobleman," said Louly. "We could play it out, I suppose. It would be good practice for me."

"And who am I, then?" inquired Poo-Bah.

"Why, you're the gypsy fortune teller, honey."

"The one with the clawlike hands?"

"That's the one. It's the best part of all, really. The whole plot hinges on her, and you can make your voice deep with doom and disaster, or you can shriek with horror and despair. Like this," said Louly, making her voice deep and resonant: " 'I read ill fortune in the cards. Things are not as they seem. All, all is lost, and bloody death is just around the corner.' " Then she raised her voice to a shrill cry: " 'Alas! Alas! We've lost our gypsy child. The lovely Zingarella is no more!' "

"Does she really say all that in the poem?" Cordy asked.

"Of course not," Louly said. "But when we play it, we have to put in a little padding."

Delighted with her part, Poo-Bah began to experiment with her voice.

"Death! Bloody death!" she groaned, "Oh, horror! Horror! Horror!"

"Fine," said Louly. "I think you've got it, honey."

"But nobody really dies in the poem," objected Chrys.

"They ought to," Cordy said. "There's nothing like a nice bloody death or two to make it exciting. I think it should be Sir Oliver Trent who dies. It can't be Amadeo because he has to be alive to marry Zingarella."

"But poor Sir Oliver has a bad enough time anyway," objected Louly. "Besides, he's really Zingarella's brother."

"Death! Death! Death!" groaned Poo-Bah happily. "Horror! Horror! Horror!"

"All right," said Chrys. "I don't mind dying if it will make a good play. I can fall down very realistically and jerk my legs a couple of times in the final agony. It'll be a nice change from always having to be the heroine."

" 'Like blades of fire the naked rapiers flew,' " quoted Louly dreamily. "Yes, we could murder Sir Oliver right there easy enough. But I really think he should live on to learn that Zingarella is his sister."

"Maybe he could die of shock when he finds out," suggested Cordy.

"I'd rather die violently," said Chrys. "I like the idea of being run through by a naked rapier like a blade of fire."

"Why don't we rewrite the whole thing?" asked Cordy.

"Listen!" said Louly. "Do I hear the lawn mower?"

They looked out of the window and saw that Ko-Ko was at work mowing the lawn. He had forgotten to put on the catch basket, and the long grass flew up in a green fountain from the whirling blades.

"He's actually working on our lawn," Louly said. "We'd better be responsible and finish up our house-cleaning."

"Oh, no, Louly, *please*! Let's go on playing Zingarella."

"Well, then, just for a few minutes before we put the crazy-quilt pieces away."

"So where do we start?"

"Let's start where Sir Oliver rides up to the gypsy camp and first sees Zingarella."

"We'll need outdoor space for that."

"Then how about the scene in the gypsy caravan? We can do that in the living room downstairs."

They trooped down to the living room, trailing their finery. Each one was trying out appropriate lines as she went.

"Ah, lovely maid, I stoop to kiss your hand," murmured Chrys, and Cordy cried, "Touch not yon gypsy maiden's raven locks!"

"Fair youth, you must not quarrel over me," intoned Louly, and Poo-Bah repeated happily, "Death! Death! Horror! Horror!"

"Now here's the gypsy caravan," said Louly, moving a few chairs to indicate four walls, "and here's a yardstick and the poker for flashing rapiers. The duel can take place just outside the caravan, and we'll play like the piano stool is the campfire."

"We really ought to do this out of doors. It would be more fun."

"Yes, but if Ko-Ko saw us doing a play, he'd stop mowing the lawn."

"All right. Indoors, then."

"Now be careful with the rapiers. We don't want anybody hurt."

"Only killed," said Chrys cheerfully.

Chrys and Cordy were in the midst of a beautiful duel, crying, "Have at you!" and "Death to the traitor!" and "Draw, dastard, draw!" when the telephone rang.

There was a sudden silence. Everybody looked at Louly and Louly turned white as a sheet. The telephone rang again, and Poo-Bah said, "Answer it, Louly! Answer it." Like a sleepwalker, Louly went to the telephone on the dining-room wall and took down the receiver.

"Yes?" she said in a small voice.

The other girls in all of their gypsy finery stood where they were, looking and listening.

"*Who?*" said Louly into the telephone. "No, you must be mistaken— Oh, wait a minute. Yes. Yes.

Miss *Permeliar* Silverbottom? Just a minute, I'll call her."

Louly put her hand over the mouthpiece of the telephone and stood looking wildly around her.

"It's Mr. Peter Spiegel. He wants Miss Silverbottom," she said. "What shall I do?"

"You told him you would call her," Cordy said.

"Use your Southern accent," Poo-Bah suggested.

"You want to go, don't you?" asked Chrys.

"Yes, I want to go," said Louly, "but this is *real*. Oh, what shall I do? This isn't play-like any more."

"Well, you can't keep him waiting," said Cordy sensibly.

Louly took her hand off the mouthpiece. Her voice sounded small and forlorn.

"I'm sorry," she said, "but Miss Permeliar Silverbottom isn't here, and Professor Tucker isn't either. I'm Professor Tucker's daughter. Can I help you?"

The gypsies, with worried faces, crowded around the telephone. They could hear a voice going tickety-tack at the other end of the line, but they couldn't make out a word that Mr. Peter Spiegel was saying.

"Yes?" said Louly. "Yes. You mean you'll let Warsaw High School enter the contest? Even if Professor Tucker and Miss Silverbottom aren't here? Even if— Yes. Yes. Of course our contestant can be there.

Right on time, yes. You want every high school in
the county represented—even if Warsaw High is
not having a summer session? Oh, good! Oh, Mr.
Spiegel, I love you! Yes. Good-by."

Louly hung up the telephone and collapsed into
the nearest chair. Now her white-as-a-sheet look
had turned to bright pink.

"Oh, I told him I loved him!" she cried. "I didn't
mean to do that. I hope he didn't understand me.
Did I mumble?"

"It was clear as a bell," said Poo-Bah.

"I don't think he'll mind," said Chrys. "People love
to be loved."

"Well, tell us! Are you going?" asked Cordy.

"Yes, I'm going," Louly said. "Mr. Spiegel is sending application blanks by the next mail. They want
every high school in the county to be represented.
He can't imagine why Warsaw High School was not
notified."

"Louly!" said Chrys. "That pile of mail on your
father's desk! Maybe the notice has been there all
the time."

"Oh, don't tell me!" Louly cried. "And I wrote that
fancy letter and everything!"

"But he'll remember you because of the letter."

"Especially since you said you loved him."

"I don't care," said Louly, "but anyway we're all

going, and it will be big and important, kidlets, it will be big!" Louly was back to her normal color now, and she was bristling with plans. "Take off all those scarves and patches and fold them neatly in the box. First of all, we'll finish the cleaning we started, just as fast as we can. Then I've got to begin work on the recitation—and I *really* mean work. No more play-like. If I'm going to represent Warsaw High School while Daddy is away, I'd better do a good job of it."

"We can finish up here, Louly," Cordy said.

"Yes," said Chrys, "go and work on the recitation, Louly. We'll leave you all to yourself, and we'll do a good job of the cleaning."

"Miss Permeliar Silverbottom isn't here," said Poo-Bah regretfully. "Good-by, Miss Silverbottom!"

13 · Journey into the Great World

"Are you sure that you have chosen the best recitation, Louly?" Aunt Eugenia asked. "It seems a little melodramatic somehow. How about 'The Village Blacksmith' or 'Thanatopsis' or 'If' or something spiritual?"

"Oh, no!" the girls all cried. "It must be 'Zingarella'!"

"You see," explained Louly, "it's the hardest one in the elocution book, and it gives the greatest range of emotions and gestures and tones of voice."

"Besides, we all love it, Aunt," said Chrys.

"Well, Louly hopes to please the judges and the audience—not just you girls. She wants to win."

"Yes, I do," said Louly, "but, honestly, Miss Eugenia, I think I can do best with 'Zingarella.'"

"All right, dear," Aunt Eugenia said. "What are you going to wear?"

"I've been thinking about that," Louly said. "I plan to make something new, something that will be appropriate."

"What, Louly?" cried the other girls. "Can we help you?"

"I have a little black bodice," Louly said, "that was part of an old costume of Mother's. It fits nicely. I know, because I've tried it. And under that I'll wear a full white blouse. And for the skirt—"

"Go on, Louly. For the skirt—"

"For the skirt, I'll sew together all the colored pieces in the crazy-quilt box and make a gypsy skirt."

"Oh, swell! Swellissimus!" cried Cordy.

Aunt Eugenia looked doubtful. "You're sure you want to do that, Louly?" she said. "You don't think that a nice simple white dress would be better? I'm sure that all the other girls in the contest will be simply dressed."

"I think that Zingarella needs an unusual dress, Miss Eugenia," said Louly, "and I really don't mind being different from the other contestants!"

"Oh, Louly!" Chrystal sighed. She felt a shudder of anxiety and apprehension going down her spine like a firelit rapier thrust. Not to mind being different! If she had been in Louly's shoes, she knew that she would have selected the simple white dress. But then she would never, never be in Louly's shoes, to stand on a platform with hundreds of people looking at her and waiting for her to remember a recitation!

Their plans went forward with all proper speed.

The girls helped Louly sew together the bands and strips of vivid color to make her gypsy skirt. They ransacked their trinket boxes for strings of colored beads for Louly to wear.

"And you must have some gold hoop earrings, Louly," Cordy said. Cordy was always an authority on costume, and Louly appreciated this.

"But where shall I get them?" she wondered.

"I know!" said Chrys. "We used to have a curtain pole in the parlor before we got the new narrow rods. In the woodshed we have a box full of wonderful brass rings that used to slip over the curtain pole to hold up the curtains. They look like gold. They'd make swell gypsy earrings. I've always wondered what we could do with them."

There were so many things to do, and so little time was left in which to do them! It was hard to sleep at night when one had to think about packing overnight bags and buying railroad tickets and getting all ready to go, even if it was only twenty miles away. But at last the day arrived, and they all went to the station and heard the train come thundering in just as it had puffed and thundered when it took Mr. and Mrs. Tucker away. Now it had come for them!

Mrs. Lark was paying the fares of Cordy and Louly and Poo-Bah, and Chrys had her allowance. The boys had mowed lawns to good purpose, and Ko-Ko, Matt, and Vince were all there, pretending to be more interested in the railroad ride than in the elocution contest. They jingled the money in their pockets and did not mind displaying it and counting it in public. They were not often so rich.

"Beware of pickpockets," Cordy said. "You go around showing your money to everyone and you'll come home without any."

"Don't worry," said Matt. "Nobody's going to trick me out of my hard-earned cash. Most of it will still be in my pocket when I come home."

"What'll you bet?" said Cordy.

"I don't bet with nice little girls like you," said Matt.

"Children!" Mrs. Lark admonished.

Twenty miles is not very far on a railroad train. But it was far enough for Ko-Ko to parade up the aisle after the conductor, pretending to punch tickets, and for Matt to impersonate the brakeman with "All aboard!" and "Watch your step!"

With some of the money he had earned pulling weeds, Vince bought a package of peppermint chewing gum from the chewing-gum machine and presented it to Poo-Bah. Cordy and Chrys winked at each other. "Poo-Bah will soon be romantical too," they giggled happily. Everybody was excited and jumping up and down to look out of the window or get a drink from the water cooler.

"What kind of a convention is this?" asked the conductor jovially.

"We're going to Springdale to see my sister win a silver loving cup," said Poo-Bah.

"You don't say! How is she going to do that?"

"She's going to be a gypsy in the speaking contest, and we are going to stay overnight in the hotel. Would you like to hear her say her piece? It's called 'Zingarella or the Gypsy Bride.' "

"Well, I'd like to," said the conductor. "How long will it take?"

"She's timed it," Poo-Bah said. "It takes about twenty minutes."

"Too bad!" said the conductor. "We'll be nine miles beyond Springdale by that time."

Everybody laughed and chattered except Louly. She sat quite still and pale with her purse and the elocution book from the library clutched firmly against her side. Her eyes had a faraway look.

"Do you have butterflies in your stomach, Louly?" Chrystal asked softly.

"It's worse than that," Louly said. "I'm scared."

After that Chrys was silent too. She had never imagined that anything would frighten Louly. It was a sobering thought to know that something could.

But when they arrived at Springdale there was no time for introspection. The station was full of young people arriving from other county towns or meeting friends and relatives. Before the train came to a complete stop they saw Eddie Wendell running along the platform with his eyes on the train windows.

"Louly, look! Wave to him. It's Eddie!"

Louly's color began to come and go again. She leaned over from the aisle where she was standing and looked out of the window. She waved and smiled. Eddie clasped his hands and shook them over his head to indicate triumph and delight.

Then they were all pushing down the aisle and down the car steps to the platform.

A tall and pleasant-looking young man stepped forward and said to Mrs. Lark, "I am Peter Spiegel, and you are Miss Silverbottom, I presume?"

"No, I am Mrs. Lark."

"Miss Permeliar Silverbottom stayed at home," shouted Poo-Bah.

"I am the mother of one of the girls, and this is our contestant, Miss Louisa Lee Tucker," Mrs. Lark said.

"Oh, Miss Louisa Lee Tucker," Mr. Spiegel said. "I'm happy to meet you. I really am."

Cordy and Chrys stared at him hard to see if he would blush as Louly was doing. But he looked quite calm. Perhaps young ladies told him over the telephone every day that they loved him.

"He's good-looking enough so they might," whispered Cordy.

But Mr. Spiegel was there to greet other people besides themselves. He was busy directing the various contestants and visitors as they arrived.

"The contest will begin at seven o'clock this evening," he said, "in the gymnasium of the high school.

It will be a long program with a good many speakers, so we plan to start promptly. If you are staying at the hotel, I advise Miss Tucker to get a little rest."

"We'll try to see that she does," said Mrs. Lark.

But that was easier said than done. Eddie Wendell had other plans for them. He had taken the afternoon off from the store, and there were tennis matches for them to watch and then they must see the town and go to the ice-cream parlor.

"All of us?" asked Poo-Bah. "Can we have ice-cream sodas?"

"Yes, everybody," Eddie said.

"Louly, wouldn't you like to rest?" asked Mrs. Lark.

"Oh, no, please," said Louly. "I couldn't sleep a wink. This will do me much more good than lying on a bed worrying."

"You are probably right," Mrs. Lark said. "But before you go out you must come up to the hotel room and unpack and hang up your dresses for this evening. Then I'll let you all go, if you're sure to be back by five o'clock."

Mrs. Lark and the girls had the largest room in the hotel, and besides the double bed there were three folding cots. The three boys had the room next door.

As soon as their Sunday dresses and Louly's

gypsy costume were shaken out and hung on hang-
ers in the closet, the girls rushed downstairs to join
the boys in the hotel lobby. There were potted palms
in the lobby and everything was on a grander scale
in Springdale than it was in Warsaw. They might
have been in Paris or London or Timbuktu instead
of only twenty miles from home.

Louly put on her Southern accent for at least five
minutes and they all stood straighter and walked
more sedately than they did in Warsaw. Eddie
wanted to show them everything about the town,
from the Spanish-American War Memorial at one
end of Main Street to the ornamental watering
trough at the other. They found themselves walking
by twos instead of in a crowd. Eddie and Louly,
Ko-Ko and Cordy, Matt and Chrys, and Vince and
Poo-Bah. In Warsaw the boys wouldn't have been
seen on the same side of the street as the girls, but
in this foreign country they were quite polite, helping the girls across intersections and taking the outside of the sidewalk to protect the girls from run-
away horses or the unpredictable new automobiles.
It was very stimulating. When they passed a drug-
store, Vince rushed in and bought Poo-Bah a package of Juicy Fruit chewing gum, and they all wound
up at the ice-cream parlor for double ice-cream
sodas. There were potted palms at the ice-cream

parlor, and Louly remembered her Southern accent for another five minutes until she began to sip her soda.

Mrs. Lark had asked Eddie to have dinner with them at the hotel, and that was exciting too. The girls all put on their Sunday dresses—even Louly, who did not wish to spoil the effect of her entry into the speech contest by appearing beforehand in her gypsy finery. There were potted palms in the hotel dining room too, but by that time Louly was too excited to bother with her Southern accent for even a few minutes.

They ordered consommé and lobster Newburg and French pastries, none of which they had ever tried before, and Poo-Bah had to stick a large wad of gum under the seat of her chair before she could begin.

"Louly," Mrs. Lark said, "I hope all of this strange food on top of ice-cream sodas and no rest will be all right for you. I wouldn't want you to get sick or anything."

"Oh, Mrs. Lark," Louly said. "I'm having such a good time. I don't think anything bad can happen to you when you're having a good time. It's only when you aren't enjoying yourself that the bad things happen."

"Well, I hope so, dear," Mrs. Lark said.

The lobster Newburg was a little strange, but the French pastries more than made up for it. They were wheeled up on a little cart by the waitress, and there were all kinds to choose from. Strawberry tarts with crinkled edges were wedged in between small chocolate cakes with whipped-cream roses, round cakes rolled in chopped nuts, and pastries oozing with custard and topped with coconut. Each one looked so good that it was hard to choose.

Poo-Bah had three and she forgot to collect her gum from under the seat of her chair when she left the dining room. But then, she had lots of gum.

After dinner there was a bustle of preparation for the speech contest. The girls and Mrs. Lark helped Louly into her gypsy costume and she looked lovely. Eddie had borrowed his uncle's horse and delivery wagon from the store to take Louly up to the high school gymnasium so that she need not walk and tire herself.

Mrs. Lark and the other six walked from the hotel. A full moon was shining in a clear sky and the crickets were chirping in the grass. Now the boys walked ahead, shoving each other and laughing. The girls walked behind with Mrs. Lark.

"I hope they know the way," Mrs. Lark said.

"Indubitably," Cordy said. "Eddie showed us this afternoon. If the boys can't find it, we can."

"I feel as if I'd lived here all my life," breathed Chrys. She looked at the moon, and she almost felt as if a poem were coming on. But she resolutely shoved the feeling down. No more poems, *please*!

The gymnasium was brightly lighted and crowds of people were streaming in.

"Eddie said to go around to the side door and we'd find some seats near to the platform that he would be saving for us," Ko-Ko said.

As they went in the side door Chrys glanced up a stairway, and through a half-opened doorway she caught a glimpse of Louly's gypsy costume. It was unmistakable among the plain white dresses of the other girl contestants. On an impulse, Chrys ran up the stairs and caught Louly's hand.

"Oh, good luck, Louly. Good luck!" she said.

"Thank you, Chrys," said Louly. "I hope I won't need it."

"You aren't scared now, are you?"

"No," said Louly, "I'm brave as a lion."

Chrys gave her hand a squeeze and ran downstairs again to join the others.

"Is she scared?" they all asked.

"No. She says she's brave as a lion, and I think she really means it."

14 · The Speech Contest

With a platform at one end and rows and rows of folding chairs, the high school gymnasium had been transformed into an auditorium. On the platform were potted palms and a row of folding chairs for the contestants. A small table in the center of the stage held a pitcher of ice water and some glasses in case the throats of the contestants became too dry for elocution. And in the center of the table was the shining silver loving cup.

Eddie had saved good seats for Louly's people, and on each seat lay a printed program with the names of the contestants and the pieces they would speak and the high schools they represented.

First of all they looked for Louly's name, and there it was:

Miss Louisa Lee Tucker
Warsaw High School
"Zingarella or the Gypsy Bride"

But it was far down on the list of twelve contestants, next to the last one.

"The audience will be all tired out before she ever gets a chance to speak," worried Chrys.

"Why didn't they put Louly first?" asked Poo-Bah.

"Well, look," said Ko-Ko. "They've put the speakers in alphabetical order according to the names of the high schools. Albion's first, then Buford and Gaultsville. Warsaw is next to the end before Youngstown. I suppose they had to have some way of deciding what order the speakers would come in."

"Then why didn't they start with Youngstown and work back?" asked Poo-Bah. "It isn't fair. I'll be sure to go to sleep before they ever get to Louly."

"We'll wake you, Poo-Bah," Chrys said. But she was already suffering agonies for Louly. To have to wait that long, listening to so many other contestants, before her turn came! To have to speak to a tired and restless audience! To have to remember that long rigmarole about Zingarella and the claw-like hands and flashing rapiers! The ice-cream sodas and consummé and lobster Newburg and French pastries that she had eaten began to churn around in Chrys's stomach and make her feel uneasy.

It was even worse when the contestants came onto the platform, for Louly was the only one in fancy costume. The boys wore blue serge suits and white shirts, and the girls wore plain white dresses that looked like a graduation or a wedding, and there was Louly as different as a thistle in a green-house of roses.

Even the names of the recitations were more conventional than Louly's. The contestant from Albion was to recite "The Village Blacksmith"; Buford had selected "Little Eva's Prayer"; Gaultsville, "Thanatopsis." Chrys ran her finger down the list: "The Wreck of the Hesperus," "If," "The Children's Hour," "Uncle Podger Hangs a Picture." Only "Zingarella or the Gypsy Bride" seemed to be in a different world.

Aunt Eugenia had been right. Louly should have worn a plain white dress and found a poem like "The Village Blacksmith" or "The Children's Hour."

What possible chance did she have of winning? In a flash Chrys saw how their little private world of play, in which rapiers flashed in the firelight and gypsy maidens turned into long-lost heiresses, was far away from solid, everyday living. All summer she and Louly and Cordy and Poo-Bah had been caught up in a delightful world of make-believe, and now in a moment of truth, in a gymnasium with creaking folding chairs and potted palms, the make-believe had suddenly evaporated. It left Louly, dear, wonderful Louly, sitting in poetic fancy dress on a platform that was pure prose, behind a pitcher full of ice water.

Chrys began to shiver as if she herself would have to get up in a moment and give a recitation before an audience of heartless and unimaginative people. She looked at Cordy, but Cordy was smiling and confident, and Poo-Bah was blissfully chewing gum.

Only Ko-Ko seemed to share Chrys's sense of unease.

"I wish she hadn't worn that crazy dress," he said.

Now Mr. Peter Spiegel strode to the center of the platform and made a short speech of introduction. He looked very handsome, and Cordy leaned over to whisper in Chrys's ear, "They say he isn't married." But in her present state of anxiety, this bit of information did not give Chrys any pleasure.

"S-s-sh!" she said.

"We are proud to welcome the twelve contestants, representing twelve high schools from twelve towns in our county. Some of you came by automobile or by horse and buggy. Some even came on the train from as far as twenty miles away."

Poo-Bah started to jump up and say, "Hooray for us!" but Cordy pulled her down.

"Our first contestant is Miss Cheryl Cox of Albion, who will recite for you 'The Village Blacksmith' by Henry Wadsworth Longfellow."

Miss Cheryl Cox was as scared as Chrystal was. Her knees knocked together and her gestures seemed to have nothing to do with the poem. Her voice was scarcely audible beyond the second row of folding chairs.

"Well, count that one out," muttered Cordy cheerfully.

"But it must be terrible to come first," whispered Chrys. "It's worse than being next to the last."

After Albion, the contestants began to improve. Each one seemed to be better than the one before.

The representative from Buford was a plump girl who spoke her lines loudly and with spirit. In the midst of "Little Eva's Prayer," she actually got down

on her knees, closed her eyes, and lifted praying
hands. Her mother, who was sitting in the first row,
began to sob and had to leave the auditorium until
she could regain her composure. There was wild
applause.

Gaultsville was a very serious boy who gave
"Thanatopsis" with deep solemnity. It was long and
there were not many gestures to relieve the general
gloom. Unfortunately, the speaker's voice was
changing, and, after rumbling along for ten solemn
minutes, it suddenly shot up on

> *"So live, that when thy summons comes to join*
> *The innumerable caravan, which moves*
> *To that mysterious realm—"*

And the recitation ended on a high and almost
comical note. Still, the applause was deafening.

But audiences soon grow weary. As the recitations continued, the applause grew gradually
weaker.

Poo-Bah put her head on Mrs. Lark's shoulder
and began to doze. Chrys had long ceased to shiver,
but she felt even more than ever that Louly's piece
was doomed.

Then when everybody was growing tired and beginning to think wistfully of home and bed, Andrew
Blunt, the contestant from Reuben's Creek, sud-

denly snapped them to attention. He was a small, red-headed boy with freckles and he had a good strong voice. He offered a comical selection called "Uncle Podger Hangs a Picture." It was not a poem and it told with humor and exaggeration of the trials of a man trying to hang a picture to suit his exacting wife. In a moment he had the audience laughing. Oh, what a relief to laugh after all the solemn caravans and orphan's prayers! When Reuben's Creek had finished, there was wild applause. Some of the boys even whistled and stamped their feet.

"There goes the silver cup," said Cordy. "I guess he is the one."

"Next time we'll see that Louly has a funny piece," whispered Chrys. She looked at Louly sitting so quiet in her gaudy dress on the folding chair beside the potted palm. Louly's hands were folded in her lap, her eyes stared straight ahead of her. There was no telling what she was thinking.

And then Mr. Spiegel said, "And now we have the contestant from Warsaw High School, Miss Louisa Lee Tucker, who will recite for you a poem called 'Zingarella or the Gypsy Bride.'"

When Louly got up, her folding chair collapsed with a loud clatter and everybody tittered. The audience was in a wonderful mood for laughing, and here was a girl dressed in a fancy costume, different from the other contestants, and her chair had collapsed. The titter rose to a sudden roar of laughter.

Chrys had begun to shiver again, and in a moment she felt sure that she would burst into tears. But Louly looked perfectly calm and composed. She came to the front of the platform and stood silently waiting for the laughter to cease. When it had almost died away, she began to smile.

"Before I begin my recitation," she said in a clear, bright voice, "I would like to say that I wore this costume to put you into the right mood for the poem. I didn't plan the sound effects, but they are appropriate, because, you see, the poem starts with a clap of thunder."

The audience laughed again, but this time they were laughing *with* Louly, not *at* her. Louly raised her hand and put a finger to her lips, and everyone was quiet. Then, in her voice that could soar with wings when she wished to make it do so, Louly began to recite.

"Loud rolled the thunder, lightning rent the sky,
  The gypsy camp in midnight darkness lay—"

Chrys could never remember afterward just how Louly had done it, with what accents of doom or shrieks of terror or simple words of moving action, with what gestures and facial contortions, or with what native charm, she had put the creaky old poem across to her audience. But when Louly finished on an almost whispered note of quietness, there was an enthusiastic burst of applause. The boys whistled and stamped even more than they had done for "Uncle Podger." Cordy and Chrys and Poo-Bah, who was wide awake now and had swallowed her gum, put their arms around each other and pounded each other on the back.

The contestant from Youngstown was an anti-climax and no one listened to him. The judges took quite a long time to confer and then they passed a paper to Mr. Spiegel and he read the results of their conference.

"The judges wish to commend the excellent performance of Mr. Andrew Blunt of Reuben's Creek for his humorous reading of 'Uncle Podger Hangs a Picture.' In their opinion, however, the first place must go to a young lady who, in spite of being rather too fussily dressed and having selected a rather too melodramatic recitation, was able to overcome the initial handicap of a collapsing chair and give us a moving and spirited performance. Miss Louisa Lee Tucker of Warsaw High School, will you please come forward and receive the silver loving cup?"

Louly got up with care, so that her chair would

not collapse again, and came forward to accept the shiny cup from Mr. Spiegel's hands. She made a lovely bow and smiled at everyone. As Mr. Spiegel handed her the cup, he turned to the audience with a grin and said: "This is the first young lady who ever told me that she loved me—over the telephone, and before she had even seen me! And a very pretty young lady too, if I may say so."

15 · Louly Is Not Embarrassed

Victory did not embarrass Louly. While the gymnasium floor was being cleared of chairs, she stood beside Mr. Spiegel at the head of the line of contestants to shake hands with people in the audience and receive their congratulations. Mrs. Lark and the girls had rushed up first to hug her and tell her how proud they were. Now they stood aside and watched while a procession of friendly well-wishers paraded by to shake Louly's hand.

"It was very well done, Miss Tucker."

"You certainly deserved the cup."

"We were hoping that you would win—yes, just as soon as your chair collapsed, we began to hope."

"Thank you," Louly said. "Thank you very much."

"She's a celebrity, Mama. Isn't she?" Cordy asked.

"Yes, she is—in a small way at least," said Mrs. Lark. "Perhaps she'll really be one in a bigger way someday."

Chrys did not say anything, but she watched Louly accepting people's praise with pride and satisfaction and being pleased and gracious. Yes, it could be done, Chrys thought. Louly was not afraid of being different. She did what she longed to do as well as she could, and when people praised her, she accepted the praise modestly but with pleasure.

Chrys thought of the torn bits of newspaper in the shoe box under her bed. But she knew that she could never be like Louly, unless . . . unless . . . .

When the floor was cleared and the chairs were pushed back against the wall, the gymnasium was suddenly transformed into a ballroom. The platform, where the speakers had stood so recently, became a place for the orchestra. A piano was pushed up beside the platform and two violinists and a cellist took their places on it. They began to play "The Merry Widow Waltz."

Eddie Wendell caught Louly about the waist and waltzed her out on the dance floor. Then everybody began finding partners and joining in the fun. Ko-Ko selected a blonde girl named Karen and Matt went whirling away with a redhead named Ginger. Vince grabbed Poo-Bah and they began to caper about at the edge of the floor in their own version of the waltz. Mrs. Lark found a seat beside some other mothers. Everybody felt well acquainted by now and introductions were unnecessary.

"Well," Cordy said to Chrys, "I guess it's the old wallflower bit for us. Remember the costume party at the Allisons'?"

"I remember."

But then two boys came sliding across the floor, dodging the dancers.

"Don't look," said Cordy, "but I think—"

One of the boys was very tall and thin, the other one was short and rather broad, but they looked nice, as well as the girls could see while pretending not to see.

"Do you want to dance?" the tall one asked Chrys.

"Well, I'm not particular," said Chrys. "Do you?"

"I'm not particular either, but I might, if you do."

"Of course she wants to dance," said Cordy. "So do I."

"Here we go, then," said the short, broad boy, whirling Cordy away with him. They would have made handsomer couples if the tall one had asked Cordy and the short one had asked Chrystal, but there is no accounting for tastes.

Cordy's new friend was named Bevis and Chrys's tall one was called Shrimp and they were going to be sophomores at James Russell Lowell High School in Springdale next year.

"What year are you at Warsaw High?" Shrimp asked.

"I'll be a freshman in the fall," said Chrys. "You see, I haven't even started high school yet. We're here because we're friends of Louisa Lee Tucker's."

"Well, you look all right," said Shrimp. "If you don't tell anyone you aren't in high school yet, they probably won't know the difference."

Chrystal felt pleased. She really was out in the big, foreign, outside world after all.

Bevis and Shrimp stuck to them for the rest of the evening. Sometimes Bevis danced with Chrys and Shrimp with Cordy. The two boys were fast friends and they sensed that Cordy and Chrys were friends too.

Once when they were standing by the punchbowl having punch, Cordy said to Chrys, "Well, this is the first time we've been on this side of the punchbowl, isn't it, Chrys?"

Chrys tried to signal Cordy to be careful what she said. But Cordy went on, "Chrys and I often serve punch at the college dances when my mother acts as patroness. Sometimes a kind soul will ask us to dance, but mostly we just have to be little girls and stand there serving punch."

"You mean this is your first regular dance?" asked Shrimp.

"Indubitably," said Cordy.

"Oh, Cordy," said Chrys, "they'll think we're awfully dumb!"

But Shrimp and Bevis were grinning and cuffing each other.

"Is it really your first dance?" asked Bevis.

"Well, you heard Cordy say it, didn't you?"

"So shall we tell them?" asked Shrimp.

"Might as well," said Bevis.

"Well, it's ours too," said Shrimp.

"No!" cried Cordy. "I thought you were men of the world."

"But you're sophomores in high school!" Chrystal cried. "We thought you were so sophisticated."

"Well, we aren't," said Bevis. "That is, yes, of course we are. But we've been too busy doing hobbies and things to care much about dancing. Do you know we've built a telephone line between our two houses?"

"You built it yourselves? How perfectly swellissimus!"

It was a wonderful evening from beginning to end. The moments of anxiety over Louly's fate only tended to sweeten the joy of her triumph and the pleasure of the dancing afterward. But the speech contest had taken a long time and the gymnasium had to be closed by midnight. Too soon the party was over.

Mrs. Lark went around saying, "Girls, girls! Time to go back to the hotel now. We have to leave early in the morning, you know."

"What time does your train leave?" asked Shrimp.

"At nine-thirty," Chrystal said.

"We'll be there," said Bevis.

Back in the hotel room it was difficult to settle down. Poo-Bah, completely exhausted, went to sleep with her best hair ribbon still tied to her hair and her teeth unbrushed.

"But with all of that gum she's been chewing, her teeth probably will be all right for one night," said Louly. "And, oh, chillun, wasn't it dreamy, creamy?"

"Yes, it was," said Chrys. "It was an adventure in the wide, wide world!"

"And do you know what Ko-Ko said about the little blonde girl he kept dancing with all evening?"

"No, what did he say?"

"He said, 'I only stepped on her feet four times, and she was so nice she never even minded'!"

"Oh, faint praise! Faint praise!" The girls dissolved into laughter.

"And do you know what the Uncle Podger boy said when he asked me to dance with him?" Louly asked.

"No, what did he say?"

"Girls! Girls!" said Mrs. Lark. "This is positively enough! I want absolute silence from now on until we can all get to sleep."

"Oh, Mama, let her tell us!"

"Not another word tonight!"

"Then tell us in the morning, Louly."

"Oh, Mrs. Lark, I won't be able to sleep a wink unless she tells us."

"Well, just tell it quickly, Louly."

"He said, oh, he said, 'Miss Tucker, I think that

you are a great artist. I was prepared to win this contest, but I gladly hand the silver loving cup to you.' "

"Oh, how magnificent of him, Louly."

"Silence, girls. Not another whisper, *please!*"

By nine o'clock the next morning the delegates from Warsaw were at the railroad station waiting for the nine-thirty train. The sleep was scarcely out of their eyes, but they did not have time to yawn because a number of Springdale people had come to see them off. It was almost as exciting as it had been the night before.

Karen and Ginger were there, and they had brought a box of cookies for Ko-Ko and Matt.

"These are to eat on the train," said Karen, and Ginger said, "We sat up half the night to make them."

"I don't see Bevis or Shrimp," said Cordy.

"Or Eddie," said Chrys. "Louly will certainly be disappointed. I don't suppose that you and I could care less, but Louly will take it to heart."

But the Uncle Podger boy from Reuben's Creek was there with a bunch of flowers, and Louly did not look as if her heart were broken.

At a quarter after nine there was a sound of running feet, and Eddie, followed by Bevis and Shrimp, came charging onto the station platform. It was almost as dramatic as the arrival of the train would be. Each one of the boys carried a box of candy.

"Sorry to be late," said Eddie, "but we had to wait until the candy store opened. This is for you, Louly, because you were so great. It's 'sweets to the sweet,' as the valentines say."

"Here," said Bevis, thrusting his box of candy into Cordy's hands.

"Take it," said Shrimp, doing the same to Chrys.

"Thank you! Thank you!" said the girls.

"Well, this is very nice, boys," said Mrs. Lark.

Ko-Ko and Matt were looking most uneasy. Suddenly they left the station platform and began to run uptown.

"Oh, *where* are they going?" cried Mrs. Lark. "The train will be here at any moment. We *can't* miss it! We can't stay over in Springdale another night!" But there was no catching them now.

The train roared into the station. The engine puffed and panted. The conductor put down his step and stood waiting for the passengers to embark. The brakeman with an oil can went along the side of the engine. The engineer looked out of his cab window and waved to them.

"Oh, what shall we do?" cried Mrs. Lark. "What shall we do?"

"They can stay overnight at my uncle's," Eddie said.

"Oh, no! Oh, no!" cried Mrs. Lark.

"Is something the matter, ma'am?" inquired the conductor.

"Two of our boys are missing," said Mrs. Lark. "They were right here, and then they vanished."

"Well, we could hold the train for a minute or two, ma'am. No longer than that."

"Please do!" said Mrs. Lark. "Please do!"

The minute or two sped by.

"Sorry, ma'am," the conductor said, "we can't wait any longer. *All aboard!*"

"Here they come! Here they come!" cried Shrimp, who was tall enough to see over the heads of the others. "They're almost here!"

"Get in, girls, for goodness' sake!" said Mrs. Lark. "Don't stand there watching for them."

The four girls and Vince clambered into the train, followed by Mrs. Lark. They crowded to the windows in time to see Ko-Ko and Matt thrusting boxes of candy into the hands of Karen and Ginger. Then the conductor gave a last call of "All aboard!" and the train began to move.

Ko-Ko and Matt caught onto the last car and swung aboard just as the train began to pick up speed.

"Oh, how exciting!" Louly cried. "What a dreamy, creamy send-off."

"Oh, Mrs. Lark, don't you *love* narrow escapes?" cried Chrys.

"Not at my age," said Mrs. Lark, wiping her brow with her handkerchief.

In a few minutes Ko-Ko and Matt came strolling into the front car from the last car of the train which they had boarded in such a hurry.

"Well, that was well timed," said Matt with satisfaction.

"I hope you didn't worry, Mrs. Lark," said Ko-Ko.

"I worried myself sick," said Mrs. Lark, "but, thank goodness, it turned out all right."

"I'll bet your pockets are empty," cried Cordy. "I'll bet you spent your last cent."

"Don't you remember?" teased Matt. "I said I never bet with little girls."

"We're big girls now," said Cordy. "Boys came to the station to see us off, and they remembered to get us boxes of candy before the very last minute."

"Children! Children! Stop bickering," said Mrs. Lark. "This candy-giving is getting to be quite an obsession. When I was a girl, it used to be flowers."

"I heard last year," said Louly dreamily, "that one of the sorority girls at the college got twenty-four pounds of candy for Christmas. Think of being so popular!"

"Did she die?" asked Poo-Bah.

"No, but I'll bet she had indigestion," offered Chrys.

"Maybe she just had a lot of younger brothers and sisters," Poo-Bah said, "who would help her eat the twenty-four pounds of candy. That's an awfully pretty box Eddie gave you, Louly."

"Don't look at it like that, Poo-Bah. I'm not going to open it until I get home, and maybe even then I won't open it, but will keep it forever as a lovely souvenir."

"Anyway, I prefer gum," said Poo-Bah. At which Vince went to the gum machine and got a package of Black Jack licorice gum which he dropped in Poo-Bah's lap. After that, whenever Poo-Bah stuck out her tongue, it was licorice-black. Poo-Bah had never had so much gum in such a short time in her life before, and she began to feel just as grown-up and romantical as the other girls with their precious boxes of candy.

The twenty miles sped by, and they were back at home. It seemed as if they had been away for weeks on an extended cruise.

16 · Emergency!

That night, before she went to sleep, Chrys sat on her cot in the sleeping porch and thought over all of her adventures. She had told and retold everything to Aunt and Grandma until she knew it by heart. Still, thinking it over was different from telling it. New facets kept cropping up in her mind.

The girls had all agreed to abandon the tent for the night, perhaps for the rest of the season, and sleep in their own beds. Chrys was suddenly glad to be alone. Much of her life she had been alone and she needed a certain amount of aloneness to be happy. During this lovely play-like summer there had been very few moments of solitude for thinking and realizing and understanding.

She looked at the unopened box of candy on the orange crate beside her bed, and *that* was something to think about, even if she never saw or heard about Shrimp again. Then she thought of Louly, standing so coolly beside Mr. Spiegel and shaking people's hands. Louly, so calm and proud and sure of herself. Louly, so wonderful!

Chrys leaned over and pulled the shoe box out from under her bed. It was the first time she had been able to look at it since the terrible Sunday when her poem had appeared.

Now she opened the box, smoothed out the crumpled newspaper, and pieced the torn parts together. The poem was childish and the drawing was crude, but it did not look as bad to her as it had at first. She trimmed off the ragged edges and folded the poem neatly away. She could even imagine that someday she might write another poem, a better one, in the old spelling tablet. A glimmer of light had begun to penetrate the darkness of her humiliation. Yes, someday, someday, she might even write a book or something that would be all printed out, and maybe she would even stand and smile when people praised her and say, "Thank you, thank you very much," instead of running away.

One day in the mail there was a fat letter from Michigan.

"*My darlings, my darlings,*" Mrs. Tucker wrote. "*We are coming home next week. Your daddy and I can hardly wait to be home again with you.*" There was much more, news about the relatives, thanks for the newspaper letter that the children had written, the time that the train would arrive, and all sorts of loving and foolish words of caution and advice.

The Tucker children jumped for joy. It had been a wonderful summer, but now they had had enough of it without their parents. They were eager for the day to come that would bring the family together again.

"But, my! There is a lot to do!" Louly said. "We've been careless about so many things. Look at the long grass grown up around the sweet peas, and the clutter the pan cupboard is in—and I think we'd better take down the tent and fill up the furnace hole."

"Oh, dear!" said Chrys.

"Couldn't we leave our camp for them to see?" asked Cordy.

"We can tell them all about it," Louly said. "But I'd like to have things all neat and tidy, just as they were when our parents left."

The boys helped strike the tent, and there was a last meal of raw fries on the furnace before the stovepipe and bricks were removed and the hole filled in.

"I don't think I like raw fries as well as I used to," Poo-Bah said, and Ko-Ko said, "It will sure be good to have some of Mother's cooking. Your cooking is very good, Louly, and it's getting better all the time, but still it's not like Mama's."

"Well, thank you for that left-handed compliment," said Louly. "Just for that I'll give you Shredded Wheat for supper."

Cordy and Chrys worked as hard as the Tuckers. The pan cupboard was straightened, the house was swept and dusted, the camping equipment was stored in the attic, the extra bedding was folded and packed away.

"Now for the grass in the sweet peas!" Louly said.

"Don't you ever get tired, Louly?"

"I have to be responsible," said Louly seriously.

"I don't plan to get responsible when I grow up," said Poo-Bah cheerfully.

"No one who chews gum ever grows up to be responsible," teased Cordy.

"Get the sickle, Ko-Ko," Louly directed. "I'll hold the long grass in bunches for you and you can cut it."

"We'll pull weeds in the bean rows," offered Chrys.

"Bring a basket, Poo-Bah, to put the grass and weeds in."

"I'm coming," said Poo-Bah, "but Mama always says 'please.' "

"Well, please, please, *please!*" said Louly impatiently. "We've got to hurry after so much play-like all summer."

Everybody hurried. The weeds and grass flew into the basket and the garden began to look as a nice garden should. Louly and Ko-Ko were halfway along the sweet-pea fence, Louly holding the bunches of long grass while Ko-Ko cut them with the sickle, when Ko-Ko suddenly gave a loud exclamation.

Glad to drop their weeding, Chrys and Cordy ran to see what had happened.

Ko-Ko was bending over Louly, who sat on the grass looking silently at her hand. She held the hand away from her, and a little fountain of red blood spurted out of it and dripped to the grass.

"I guess—I've cut myself," she said.

"I did it," Ko-Ko said. "I didn't mean to, though. The sickle was sharp. Her hand got in the way."

They were all frozen to the spot, watching the little fountain of blood and wondering what to do next. Suddenly Poo-Bah knew.

"Emergency! Emergency!" she shouted and began to run for Aunt Eugenia as fast as she could go.

Dripping with blood, Louly was rushed to Chrystal's house. Miss Eugenia had been trained as a nurse, and now she grabbed towels and bandages and poured antiseptic into a bowl of warm water.

"Put your hand in the water, Louly," she said. "It will sting at first, but soon the blood should stop flowing. If it doesn't, we'll make a tourniquet and call Doctor Barnes. Chrystal, get the smelling salts out of the bathroom cupboard. Louly may begin to feel faint, losing all that blood."

Chrys ran for the smelling salts. As soon as Ko-Ko had delivered Louly into Aunt Eugenia's hands he turned and went out the side door. He looked as if he had been condemned to be hanged.

They were in the dining room, and Aunt made Louly sit down with her hand in the bowl of water. Chrys came back with the smelling salts and joined

Cordy and Poo-Bah, who were standing as close as they could get to see everything that went on.

Louly's blood continued to flow.

"How do you feel, Louly?" asked Cordy.

"Fine," said Louly. She looked pale but undismayed. "I didn't know I had such red blood. Blue blood is much more elegant, I believe."

"Here," said Aunt Eugenia, "let me put a little pressure on your wrist, Louly, and see if that will stop the bleeding."

Chrys stood looking at the blood, the terribly red, running blood—and Louly was making jokes about it! Suddenly it seemed to Chrys that the room was beginning to turn around her in a very curious way. First her knees began to knock and then the starch seemed to go out of all her bones. Her head swam.

Without saying a word, she staggered to the old leather couch that occupied one wall of the dining room. Very slowly and gently she collapsed upon it and closed her eyes.

When she opened them again, Cordy was holding the smelling salts under her nose, and Louly was saying in surprise, "Why, what's the matter with Chrys? She's white as a sheet."

"Chrystal has a good imagination," Aunt Eugenia said. "I think she was suffering for you, Louly."

Chrys sat up in dismay. She was terribly

ashamed of herself, but her head was still whirling and she couldn't think of a word to say.

"Chrys has a very sensitive soul," said Poo-Bah, "as sensitive as mine, I think."

"Well, we've got the blood stopped now, dear," Aunt Eugenia said. "The cut is really not very deep and I think we've cleaned the wound sufficiently. Now for a lot of nice sterile bandage. You'll look very impressive with your hand all bandaged up."

"Oh, dear!" said Louly. "There's still a lot to be done."

"Louly!" said Aunt Eugenia. "You've done a wonderful job of getting your place ready for your parents. It looks lovely. Tonight you and Ko-Ko and Poo-Bah can have supper with us, and tomorrow, when your parents come, I'll send over a hot casserole and a custard pie. You don't need to do another thing."

"Oh, thank you, Miss Eugenia!"

"And now," said Aunt, "if Chrystal feels like getting up, we'll put Louly onto the couch with a blanket to keep her warm, and let her rest for a while."

Just then Ko-Ko came onto the side porch and leaned against the screen door, shading his eyes to look inside.

"How *is* she?" he asked anxiously.

"Do you mean Chrystal or Louly?" inquired Poo-Bah wickedly.

"I mean Louly," he said. "I ran all the way to the doctor's office and he was out. Is she going to recover?"

"I'm fine," said Louly, "and it wasn't your fault, Ko-Ko. I never should have held the grass like that with you cutting so near."

"I made the sickle real good and sharp," Ko-Ko said. "I'll go and finish the job myself now."

"Well, take care," Aunt Eugenia said. "I'm nearly out of bandages and I don't want another patient today."

"Yes, ma'am," Ko-Ko said.

When Louly was installed on the couch with Grandma's napping blanket spread over her, Cordy said, "Let's play like Louly is the victim of a railroad disaster, or shall it be that she fell off a mountain in the Alps? And we are all her rescuers and—"

"Can't you rest a minute without having to play like something?" Aunt Eugenia asked. They looked at her in amazement. Even Louly was surprised.

"Why, that's all right, Miss Eugenia," she said. "I love to play-like. It won't do me a bit of harm."

The next day Louly found a winter mitten to cover her hand so that the bandage would not be the first thing her parents saw when they arrived on the train.

"I think it's kind of a good thing we had an emergency," Poo-Bah said. "After all the talking everybody did, it would be too bad not to have one."

"But aren't you glad it wasn't *you* who had it?" Chrystal asked.

Of course Cordy and Chrys went to the station to see the train come in.

"Maybe we should leave it all in the bosom of your own family," Chrys said doubtfully.

"No," said Louly, "after all we have done together this summer, we're like one family. You and Cordy must come too."

As they stood on the platform waiting for the train, Chrys had a moment of sadness.

"Just think," she said. "Now our lovely play-like summer is over and done for."

"No," said Louly. "Nothing lovely is over and done for until the last person who remembers it forgets."

"We'll remember," the others said.

"Besides," said Louly, "I've been thinking, now that we know how to cook, we can give a formal dinner for our parents and Mr. and Mrs. Lark and Miss Eugenia and Grandma. Chrys and I will be the

Honorable Mr. and Mrs. Oswald Mortimer Montague and Cordy and Poo-Bah can be the butler and maid. We'll all share in the cooking."

"Shall we have raw fries?" asked Poo-Bah.

"No!" everybody shouted.

"We'll have creamed chicken and peas in patty shells and baking-powder biscuits with baking powder—"

"And French pastry!" said Cordy.

"If we can find a recipe. And then, I was thinking, after school starts and Eddie and all our friends come back, we might give a real play with costumes and footlights and everything—"

"Where, Louly, where?"

"Maybe in Chrys's barn loft—"

The rest of Louly's idea was drowned in the noise of the arriving train. They ran along the platform, looking in the windows, and there were Mr. and Mrs. Tucker looking out and waving and smiling. This time there were no tears. Everybody was smiling.